The Trouble
with Cupid

The Trouble with Cupid

Laura Langston

Fitzhenry & Whiteside

Published in Canada by Fitzhenry & Whiteside,
195 Allstate Parkway, Markham, Ontario L3R 4T8

Published in the United States by Fitzhenry & Whiteside,
311 Washington Street, Brighton, Massachusetts 02135

www.fitzhenry.ca   godwit@fitzhenry.ca

10 9 8 7 6 5 4 3 2 1

Library and Archives Canada Cataloguing in Publication

Langston, Laura, 1958-
The trouble with Cupid / Laura Langston.

ISBN 978-1-55455-059-3

I. Title.

PS8573.A5832T76 2008   jC813'.54   C2008-900417-5

**U.S. Publisher Cataloging-in-Publication Data
(Library of Congress Standards)**

Laura Langston
Perfect Blue / Laura Langston.
[240] p. : cm.
Summary: When a dog food company announces a competition to find a
talented dog for their ad campaign, experienced dog trainer Erin agrees to
work with the school entry: a lazy, gluttonous bulldog named Cupid.
She must succeed; otherwise she'll never be embraced by the in-crowd
or win the heart of the cutest guy in school.

ISBN-13: 978-1-55455-059-3

1. Self-perception — Fiction. 2. Dogs — Fiction. I. Title.

[Fic] dc22   PZ7.L3647Tr 2008

Fitzhenry & Whiteside acknowledges with thanks the Canada Council for the
Arts, and the Ontario Arts Council for their support of our publishing program.
We acknowledge the financial support of the Government of Canada through
the Book Publishing Industry Development Program (BPIDP) for our publishing activities.

Canada Council   Conseil des Arts
for the Arts   du Canada

ONTARIO ARTS COUNCIL
CONSEIL DES ARTS DE L'ONTARIO

Design by Fortunato Design Inc.
Cover image by Peter Hudecki

Printed in Canada

Acknowledgments

In memory of Sandy Watson,
first star on the left, Heaven

Chapter One

"JUST WALK OVER to Zach's table and sit down like you belong," Rachel told Erin as they picked up trays and took their place in line. "If you want him to notice you, you've got to make the effort." It was noon; the cafeteria at Carson Heights Junior High was filling up. But some seats were still left at Zach Cameron's table, including one right beside him.

"Easy for you to say." Erin watched Zach laugh with Suze Shillington. Suze was gorgeous. So was Rachel. Her best friend had been accepted within days of starting grade eight at their new school. As usual. "He doesn't know I'm alive."

Rachel flipped her blonde hair back and stood on her toes to glimpse the menu. "Do what I say and before you know it, you'll be hanging out with him all the time and he'll be asking you out."

"Shhhh!" Erin glanced nervously over her shoulder. There were tons of people around, including Mr.

Mean, Deryk Latham. And Erin didn't want him hearing that her big goal in life was getting Zach Cameron to ask her out.

Correction: getting Zach Cameron to say more than four words to her so he might *consider* asking her out.

"Follow the Rule of Five!" Rachel said. "Look. Talk. Ask. Laugh. Touch. It's a no-brainer."

The Rule of Five went back years. Because Rachel had been boy-crazy for years. Erin could recite the rules in her sleep. *Look Zach in the eye. Talk to him. Ask him questions. Laugh at his jokes. Touch his arm.* "It's so fake."

"No it isn't. You want a guy, you have to fight for him."

Now that she was going out with Anthony Oresti, Rachel wanted to hook Erin up with a boyfriend of her own. The only boy Erin was even remotely interested in, however, was Zach Cameron. Except every time she tried to talk to him, her tongue twisted up and practically choked her.

"Zach and I don't have classes together."

"But you're both on the Special Events Committee. Don't you talk to him then?"

"I've had extra shifts at the SPCA. I've missed the last few meetings."

Rachel pursed her lips. "How will you get a guy if you keep hanging out with dogs?"

A burst of laughter interrupted them. Down the line, Alexander Richfield squawked like a chicken; Myles Scott mooed like a cow. "Compared to most of the guys around here," Erin said dryly, "dogs are way more intelligent."

Rachel giggled. "Wanna bet there's chicken or beef on the menu?" She was right. Today's specials were barbecued chicken and chili. Rachel selected a plate of chicken legs and a bowl of salad.

"It was okay last year when I saw Zach walking his dog on Grand Boulevard." Erin put a peanut butter and jelly sandwich on her tray and picked up a carton of milk. "Then we could talk about our dogs." Zach had an Irish setter named Lucille. His dog was sweet, but Zach was sweeter. He was hot and funny and even a little bit taller than she was. "But now that he's on the soccer team, he doesn't walk Lucille anymore. And whenever I see him, he's always surrounded by his friends. I never know what to say."

"Ask him about Irish setters," Rachel suggested. "Tell him you have a friend who wants to buy one."

"That's a lie!"

Rachel grinned at the look of horror on Erin's

face. "It's no more a lie than you putting makeup on at school where your mom can't see it."

"*That's* not lying, but pretending I have a friend who wants an Irish setter *is*." She gave Rachel a pleading look. "I can't do that." Lying sent a prickly, red flush up the back of Erin's neck. It made her voice quiver; it left a queasy feeling in the pit of her stomach.

"Yes, you can." Reaching the cashier, Rachel dug into her pocket for change. "And it's not lying. It's being creative. Everybody should have an imaginary friend. I have one. Her name's Bree. Every time I want Anthony to do something nice for me, I tell him what Bree's boyfriend does for her. It's amazing how fast he comes around. You have an imaginary friend too. Her name's Lola." She waited while Erin paid.

"*Lola*?"

"Uh-huh." Rachel nodded as she led the way to Zach's table. "Lola lives on the island. Near your grandma. And she loooooves Irish setters."

Zach looked up as they approached. "Who loves Irish setters?"

Erin was amazed he could hear anything over the noise. There was his best friend Steve. Plus Nathan and Eric. Madison and Suze. Krista and Becky. All the popular kids in her grade. They were talking about fund-raising options for the spring dance.

"Erin's friend Lola." Rachel sat down across from him. That left two seats way at the end or one seat beside Zach. Rachel motioned her to the closest seat.

She didn't want to sit down. She wanted to run. Maybe to Siberia. Or the Australian outback. She didn't want to talk to Zach Cameron in front of everybody.

If you want him to notice you, you've got to make the effort, Rachel had said.

Erin sat down.

"Lola lives on Vancouver Island," Rachel said. "Near Erin's grandma. Right, Erin?"

"Right." Erin heard the quiver in her voice. Had anybody else noticed? Their conversation had died. They were looking at her. She unwrapped her sandwich, took a bite.

Suze gave Erin an amused glance. "That's the grandma who breeds three-legged dogs, right?"

Everybody laughed. Erin grew hot.

"I saw you walking it on Grand Boulevard," Suze continued. "Then Rachel mentioned you'd gotten a dog from your grandma's kennel, I kind of put two and two together. I mean two and *one* together." She giggled. "At least somebody gave the poor thing a home."

Blue wasn't a poor thing, Erin thought, opening her carton of milk. Mr. Lavender Blue, her black Flat-Coated retriever, had once been her grandmother's prized show dog. He'd lost his leg in an accident—an accident Erin had been partly responsible for. After that had happened, she'd brought Blue home to North Vancouver. Not because she felt sorry for him, but because she loved him. Trust Suze to make fun.

Erin felt Zach looking at her. "Does Lola have an Irish setter?" he asked.

She glanced sideways. His eyes were gold flecked, rimmed with chocolate brown lashes. Almost too pretty to be real. "No."

Rachel frowned.

"She had one once," Erin added. "A long time ago. When she was a baby. But it died."

Rachel's frown deepened.

"But she wants to get another one."

Rachel's frown faded; she nodded happily. Zach leaned closer. He had a tiny scar at the corner of his mouth. Who knew?

"Does she want a male or a female?"

The red flush started at the back of Erin's neck. What had she gotten herself into? "I…uh…a female."

"She wants to breed them," Rachel added helpfully.

"Really?" Zach raised an eyebrow. "And she hasn't had one since she was a baby?"

Erin knew that made no sense at all. Most breeders lived with a certain kind of dog for years before breeding them. But Rachel didn't know that. "Oh, Lola knows a lot about dogs," Rachel continued. "She's trained with them for years, right, Erin?"

"Right," Erin lied reluctantly.

"Lola helped Erin train Blue for the dog ring," Rachel said cheerfully. "She taught her a pile of tricks about working with dogs, didn't she, Erin?"

"A few, I guess." Praying Zach wouldn't ask her to explain, Erin steered the conversation to safer ground. "But Lo-ola." Her tongue tripped over the name. "Lola really likes setters." Getting the lie out was harder than squeezing toothpaste out of an empty tube.

"She has good taste." Zach took another bite of chili.

"Of course she does!" Rachel was determined to keep the conversation going. "Tell Zach why Lola likes setters so much, Erin." She picked up a chicken leg, bit into it.

Erin wanted to kill Rachel. And the moment they were alone, she would. "Setters are her favorite breed because...uh..." She searched desperately for something special to say. "Because...uh...red's her favorite color."

Lame, lame, lame!

But Zach was looking at her, listening to her, paying *attention* to her.

"And Lola likes the fact that setters are lively but good-natured. And she loves grooming so the feathered coat won't be a problem either." Erin was amazed at how easily the lies tumbled out, one on top of another. Maybe because she was talking about dogs, one of her favorite subjects. "Except...well... she's having a hard time finding one so it'll probably be a year or two before she gets one. Right now she's happy to just talk about Irish setters. To you." Erin blushed. "I mean, to me. To me from you. If you tell me stuff, I'll tell her, I mean."

Oh, God. Shut up! She stuffed her peanut butter sandwich in her mouth. She just couldn't lie.

"Hey, talk about timing!" Zach pulled a scrap of paper out of his pocket and scribbled down some numbers. "Lucille's having pups this summer. We're looking for good homes. Tell Lola to give me a call. I'd like to talk to her. See what she's looking for."

Rachel gave her a panicked look. The prickle at the back of Erin's neck spread across her shoulders, down her back. "That...uh...might be tough. For her to call, I mean."

Zach frowned. "Why?"

Why? *Why?* "Well, uh…Lola's…uh—mute!" Erin blurted. *About as mute as you could get.* "She doesn't…uh…talk to anybody she doesn't know well."

Rachel giggled nervously. "You mean, anybody at *all*, right, Erin? Being that she's mute and stuff!"

"Right." *Oh my God, let me die now!*

Perplexed, Zach glanced from Rachel to Erin. "So how do *you* talk to her?"

How *did* she talk to her? Erin's stomach took a queasy dip. She didn't talk to her. Because Lola didn't *exist*!

"They talk on the computer." Rachel came to her rescue. "Right, Erin?"

Erin attempted a smile. "Right," she said again.

"And when they're together it's not so hard because Erin knows sign language," Rachel added.

Sign language? Erin glared at Rachel. Maybe she wouldn't wait until they were alone to kill her!

"Really?" Zach looked impressed. "My mom taught sign language for years." He grinned. "She tried to teach me but I couldn't sit still long enough." He held out the slip of paper. "Get Lola to email me. Maybe we could meet. Mom's over on the island a lot. I could go with her."

Erin wanted to die right on the spot. In front of Zach Cameron and all his friends. "Sure," she said weakly. Ignoring Rachel's touch rule, Erin carefully avoided Zach's fingers as she took the paper and tucked it into her pocket.

"Hey, did you guys hear?" Madison yelled out. "Ratman's making an announcement this afternoon. Rumor is the spring dance is going to be cancelled."

Loud voices erupted all at once.

"What a drag."

"That guy should go back to his cave."

"He wants Carson Heights to be a no-fun zone."

Ratman was Mr. Ratzka, principal of Carson Heights. The man everyone loved to hate.

"Really?" The word flew out of Erin's mouth along with a scattering of bread crumbs. Embarrassed, she put down her sandwich. "What's going on?"

Zach leaned close, whispered in her ear. "Top secret. Too bad you missed the last few committee meetings."

He'd noticed!

"But don't worry. He won't cancel the dance," Zach added. "Ratzka's got something going. Just make sure you don't skip today's assembly." He winked at her. Erin's heart flew up past Mars.

Cupid tore into the cafeteria at that precise moment.

"Good grief," Rachel said with a hoot of laughter. "Look. Can you believe that?"

Erin was still digesting the fact that Zach Cameron had actually winked at *her*. And whispered in her ear. She didn't want to look at anything. But the screaming and the laughter brought Erin crashing down to earth.

Cupid, the mascot of Carson Heights, had raced into the kitchen and grabbed a barbecued chicken leg from the warming tray. With his prize clenched proudly between his teeth, the bulldog now ran in circles around the cafeteria. When someone came close, he took off in the other direction, all overbite, wrinkles, and attitude.

"Chicken on the run," someone yelled.

"Stop him!" cried Miss Pickering as she ran after him. Running being an operative word, since Miss Pickering was older than God and had a bad case of arthritis. "If he eats that chicken, it'll kill him!" the school secretary yelled.

"We should be so lucky," Suze drawled.

Nathan snorted. "Yeah. Then maybe we could get a good-looking mascot instead of one with an eating disorder."

Everyone but Erin laughed. Sure, Cupid was overweight. The dog ate everything in sight. But chicken bones were dangerous. They could stick on their way down. Or they could splinter, puncture an organ, and cause internal bleeding.

"We have to get that away from him." Erin looked at Zach for confirmation. But Zach was laughing too.

Erin stood and grabbed the crust from her peanut butter sandwich. The dog ran up the center aisle of the cafeteria and skirted the kitchen before heading to the corner of the room.

As she got close, Erin noted the amused expression in Cupid's brown eyes. He was enjoying this!

"This is a game to you, isn't it, boy? A game." She crouched down and waved the crust from her sandwich. She saw Miss Pickering out of the corner of her eye. A couple of students edged closer. Erin prayed they wouldn't startle Cupid and make him swallow the chicken.

"Trade you," she whispered.

Cupid slowed. His nose twitched. His eyes widened. The dog was obsessed with peanut butter. He adored it so much he'd been known to open backpacks to get at peanut butter sandwiches. "Come on, boy. Drop the stupid old chicken leg. Have the peanut butter instead."

Just when Erin was sure Cupid would cooperate,

someone pounced on him. Yelping, Cupid dropped the chicken leg, flung himself at Erin, and knocked her off balance. His wet nose rooted around in her hand for the peanut butter crust.

"Got it!" Deryk Latham grinned and held the chicken leg above his head.

Great, Erin thought as Cupid bolted for the door. She scrambled to her feet. The bulldog had been saved by the meanest guy in the whole school.

"Hey," drawled a familiar voice. "We didn't know you were a dog whisperer." It was Suze Shillington. Along with Madison. Nathan. Zach and Rachel.

"Of course she's a dog whisperer," Rachel came up and handed Erin her carton of milk. "She learned from her friend Lola."

Oh man. Not that again.

"Don't miss today's assembly then," Zach said as Suze tucked her arm through his elbow and prepared to lead him away. "We're going to need a good dog whisperer around here."

Chapter Two

"**D**OG WHISPERER? What were you thinking!???"

Giggling, Rachel pushed her through the doors of the gym. "You want to be part of Zach Cameron's crowd, then you've got to stand out. Be *interesting*," she stressed. "Besides, it's no big deal."

It was a big deal. She had an imaginary *mute* friend named Lola; she was an expert in sign language; and now she was a *dog whisperer*? Being around Rachel was dangerous. She followed Rachel past the bleachers. "We need to talk."

But a million other people needed to talk to Rachel too.

First it was Becky, then Krista, then Anthony. Grade eight at Carson Heights was just like elementary school. Her best friend was still the popular one and Erin was still along for the ride. Only now she was a liar on top of everything.

Tapping the microphone, Mr. Ratzka called them to order. "Take your seats please."

Erin pulled Rachel into the first two vacant seats she saw. Okay, maybe it wasn't exactly like elementary school. There were a lot more students here. And Mr. Ratzka was way stricter than Mr. Kerby, the principal at her old school.

Plus, *finally*, she was at the same school as Zach Cameron.

"You've gotta stop making things up," Erin told Rachel. "I'll never remember everything."

"You worry too much." Rachel turned around to talk to Madison.

Somebody had to worry. Besides, she only worried about things worth worrying about. Like her supposedly mute friend. And Zach's comment about needing a good dog whisperer. She watched him walk over and sit down in the front row. What was *that* about?

Mr. Ratzka cleared his throat. The murmuring in the gym faded to a whisper. "First, an announcement. A set of keys has gone missing. They're on a green ring with a large sailing medallion. They belong to our custodian. If you find them, please return them to the office immediately."

He cleared his throat a second time. "As you know, school funds are low because of our renovations. This has left the spring dance in question."

Voices rose in disappointment. "It's not totally hopeless." He put on his glasses, picked up a piece of paper. "The Woofer's Dog Food Corporation has announced a nationwide competition to find the new face of CheeseBarkers. Schools across the country are invited to submit one dog for consideration. The winning dog will have his or her face on every bag and can of CheeseBarkers Dog Food produced over the next three years. And the winning school will receive $5,000, plus a cameo appearance in the next music video produced by Tawp Dawg."

A roar went up from the crowd. "Can you believe it??!!" Rachel squeezed Erin's arm. "We could *see* Caden Vaughan!" She whirled around to talk to Madison. Tawp Dawg was the new music sensation from Wales. Their lead singer, Caden Vaughan, was always on the cover of one teen magazine or another. Erin loved their music. But she also loved the idea of Blue being the new face of CheeseBarkers!

When the talking faded, Mr. Ratzka continued. "If we participate and if we win, I'm prepared to allocate $1,500 of the $5,000 to the spring dance. The remaining $3,500 would help update our computer lab." He cleared his throat. "How many people want to select a dog from Carson Heights to enter the New Face of CheeseBarkers Contest?"

The students erupted into whistles and yells. "I take it that's a yes?" The yelling grew louder. Mr. Ratzka grinned. "Then I'll turn the rest of this assembly over to Zach Cameron, the president of the Special Events Committee."

Zach bounded onto the stage and set up a flip chart. Erin's breath caught in her throat. *We're going to need a good dog whisperer around here.*

Zach grabbed the microphone. "Here's the deal. Carson Heights has to submit a dog to the Woofer's Corporation within two weeks. We'll nominate a few dogs today. On Friday, we'll vote and choose one dog. That dog will be sent to the competition to see if he or she makes the short list."

Mr. Ratzka leaned over and whispered something to Zach.

Zach turned back to the microphone. "We won't send the actual winning dog." He grinned. "We'll produce a video of him doing his stuff. And write a letter about why he's the best."

Erin had to nominate Blue!

"One thing," Zach added. "You can't nominate your own dog. Someone else has to. And if someone nominates your dog and you disagree, you can refuse. But if you accept the nomination, you have from now until Friday to convince everyone to vote for your dog. You can do posters, talk to people, bribe them, whatever." Mr. Ratzka glared; Zach chuckled. "Okay, maybe not bribe them."

A voice came from the front row. "I'd like to nominate Lucille." It was Suze Shillington. Erin just knew she was batting her stupid long eyelashes 200 miles an hour. "Your dog, Zach."

"I second that." It was Nathan. Erin recognized his voice too.

Zach turned pink. Erin could see it even from twenty rows back. How cute was that?!

"I'll accept the nomination." He wrote *Lucille* on the flip chart and then turned back to the crowd.

Two more dogs were nominated and seconded, but both times the owners withdrew the names.

Erin leaned close to Rachel. "I want you to nominate Blue."

Rachel gasped. "I can't do that. He has three legs."

"So what?"

"He's handicapped."

"And your point is?"

"He'll never win."

"You don't know that."

"Well, yeah, I do know that. Face it, Erin. You don't show him anymore. Three-legged dogs aren't exactly show ring material."

"We're not talking the show ring. We're talking the new face of CheeseBarkers. All dogs have to eat. Even handicapped ones."

Onstage, Zach added a second name: Patches, the dog belonging to Anthony Oresti and his twin, Joseph. Patches was a lovable old mutt with one eye and bad skin.

Blue was way better than him! She elbowed Rachel. "Come on. Nominate Blue for me."

Rachel crossed her arms. "No."

"You love Blue."

"Yeah, so? That doesn't mean he's the right dog for this."

Erin's temper flared. "You made me lie to Zach. You gave me a mute friend. You turned me into a dog whisperer, and now you won't do this for me?"

Rachel refused to meet her eyes.

"If you don't, I'll tell Anthony that Bree doesn't exist."

Rachel's eyes widened. "You wouldn't."

"I would."

Scowling, Rachel put up her hand. "I nominate Mr. Lavender Blue. Blue for short. Owned by Erin Morris." She slumped down in her seat and muttered, "He's never going to win."

"And thanks for your support," Erin muttered back.

25

"Do I have a seconder?" Zach asked.

Silence.

"A seconder," he called again.

"Me. I second Blue."

It was Deryk Latham. Coming to her rescue. Again. Erin's face flamed. He'd spent all of last year embarrassing her, calling her and Rachel Beauty and the Beast. Was this another one of his tricks? She waited for him to yell out that he was kidding, but he didn't. Zach wrote Blue's name on the flip chart.

"Final call for nominations," Mr. Ratzka proclaimed.

"I nominate Cupid," someone yelled from the back row.

Groans and laughter mingled together. Someone gave a wolf whistle.

"I second it," someone else called.

Zach chuckled but made no move to write the dog's name down. Mr. Ratzka leaned over to the microphone. "That's a fine idea. After all, Cupid is the mascot of Carson Heights."

Miss Pickering nodded so fast Erin thought she might get whiplash. Zach wrote Cupid's name down. Then Mr. Ratzka declared, "Nominations are now closed."

Madison leaned forward, whispered something

in Rachel's ear. Erin caught the phrase "a pile of losers." Both girls dissolved into giggles.

"We also need some volunteers to work with the winning dog," Zach said. "Get him ready for the competition and help make the video."

Erin's hand flew into the air. So did about fifty others. Zach grinned. "I'll put a sign-up sheet outside the office. A couple of quick things. Thursday afternoon, the owners of the nominated dogs will come to the office and give two-minute speeches over the intercom on why their dog should represent Carson Heights in the competition."

A speech???? She'd rather swim with a school of man-eating sharks than speak in public.

"Voting will take place in the gym Friday," Zach continued. "All ballots must be in by noon. The winning dog will be announced at the end of the day. And the CheeseBarkers Competition Committee will hold its first meeting Saturday."

Yikes! Saturday she volunteered at the SPCA. "I'll need to change my shift," she told Rachel as they headed for the doors. But Rachel was too busy talking to Madison about Tawp Dawg and Caden Vaughan to respond.

"That's not a lot of choice," Erin heard a girl behind her remark.

27

"No kidding," a guy responded. "Once you rule out the gimped-up cripple, the mutt that smells, and the corpulent cupid, the only choice is Lucille."

Great, Erin thought. Suze had obviously told the whole world about Blue.

"Yeah, if we want to win the CheeseBarkers competition, Lucille is it."

Not true, Erin said silently. Blue had won before and he'd win again. He'd be perfect as the new face of CheeseBarkers. She just had to convince the rest of Carson Heights.

———————————— • ⬯

"How about some quinoa, Erin?" Her mother held up the pilaf.

"I'm good, thanks." Erin grinned across the table at her dad. Mom had been on a quinoa kick for weeks. She claimed the ancient Inca grain was an all-natural nutritional powerhouse. Erin bit into her spicy teriyaki salmon. Call anything "all natural" and her mother got sucked right in. Including yucky quinoa.

"So I'll switch my shift at the SPCA to Friday night this week." Erin had told her parents all about Blue trying out for the CheeseBarkers competition. "Richard said it was okay as long as I don't make a habit of it."

"Are you sure entering him is a good idea?" her mother asked.

People had been making fun of Blue all year and she was tired of it. "Just because he has three legs shouldn't matter!" She glanced at Blue waiting patiently on his mat for them to finish dinner. "Blue would be perfect as the new face of CheeseBarkers!"

At the mention of his name, he thumped his tail against the floor and gave a little whine.

Her mother smiled gently. "That's not what I meant, Erin. I meant the competition itself. Do you have time for it?"

Erin knew she was thinking about her math mark. "I'm doing better in algebra." She buttered a warm bread roll.

"It's not just algebra," her father added. "You've got strings Wednesday and the SPCA all day Saturday. The deal was you could do those extra things if they didn't interfere with your schoolwork." He scooped up the last of his salad. "Same goes for the Cheeseburgers competition."

"CheeseBarkers." The tang of warm bread and butter filled her mouth.

"Whatever. Same rules apply." Mom nodded her agreement. "Grade eight has been a tough adjustment for you," he added. "We want you to have a good year, that's all."

Grade eight *had* been a tough adjustment, mainly

because Rachel had found a new crowd of friends. Suze and Madison and Krista, and lately even Zach and his buddies. Rachel had tried to include Erin, but she'd had been left out a lot of the time. Winning the CheeseBarkers competition would change everything.

"Do you know how many handicapped dogs end up on cans of dog food?" she asked her parents.

"None," her father said.

"Exactly! Blue would be the first. Do you know how many cats and dogs we get in to the SPCA that can't be adopted because they've been injured?" Her parents shrugged. "Tons. If Blue wins—*when* he wins—people will figure out that a handicapped dog is just as lovable as a fully functioning one. They'll see that Blue is perfect just the way he is!"

A slow grin spread across her mother's face. "So you want Blue to become the face of animal rights?"

Mostly, she wanted the kids to accept Blue. Plus, if her dog won $5,000 for Carson Heights, she'd be part of the in crowd for sure! But she couldn't tell her mother that. "Maybe. I don't know." She scooped up the last of her salmon. "If we win, we'll have enough money for the spring dance." *And Zach will know I'm alive!*

"You're going to have to run a top-notch campaign," her mom added.

"I know," Erin said. "I have to write a speech. And do posters. I scanned Blue's picture, but I need a slogan to run across the top. And I'll need to get copies made. They're opening the school early tomorrow so we can put up posters."

"Who's helping you?"

"Rachel promised to show up but she wasn't too crazy about the idea." Understatement of the year. Rachel hated mornings, and she didn't think Blue stood a chance, either.

"A slogan, huh?" Her mom gazed off into the distance. "How about, 'All dogs have rights, even disabled ones.'"

"No, no." Her dad shook his head. "You can't ignore Blue's disability, but this is about Cheese-Barkers, remember? Erin has to convince people that Blue *is* the new face of CheeseBarkers."

A tiny frown puckered her mother's forehead. "What about, 'Hobble along with the right choice. Let Blue pull through for CheeseBarkers'?"

"Too negative," her father said.

"Besides, Blue doesn't hobble," Erin said hotly. "And 'let Blue pull through' makes him sound like a wimp. Blue may limp but he's no wimp!"

Her father stared at her. Then he said, "There's your slogan."

After a second, Erin grinned. "He may limp but he's no wimp." Her grin widened. "He's the new face of CheeseBarkers!"

Chapter Three

ERIN WAS WAITING OUTSIDE Carson Heights when the custodian opened the door at eight o'clock the next morning. She hurried inside to the main bulletin board by the office. After tacking up her poster, she stood back to admire it. Blue's dark fur stood out against the red background. He stared straight into the camera. Big white letters framed him. "He may limp, but he's no wimp. He's the new face of CheeseBarkers."

The next stop was the bulletin board outside the cafeteria. That's when she heard the others running up and down the hall laughing and putting up their own posters.

Where was Rachel?

"Good morning, Erin."

"Good morning, Miss Pickering."

Erin caught a whiff of lavender cologne as the secretary placed a poster of Cupid beside Blue. "Isn't he gorgeous?" she asked with a sigh.

Gorgeous wasn't the word Erin would have chosen. Cupid was barking in the picture, which made his normally wrinkled face look even more twisted. Beneath his chin, Miss Pickering had written the words, "I bark for CheeseBarkers."

"Gorgeous," Erin repeated politely.

The older lady regarded Erin with concern. "Now, dear, I know you want your own dog to win. But remember, Cupid is the mascot of Carson Heights." She leaned over to touch Erin's arm; the lavender smell grew stronger. "He'll get lots of votes and…well, I don't want you to be upset by that."

Erin smiled. "I'll be fine."

Miss Pickering seemed truly worried about her. And truly convinced that Cupid had a chance! Poor Miss Pickering.

Erin still had more than a dozen posters to put up. She flew down the halls, expecting to run into Zach and his crew or the Oresti twins, who were lobbying for Patches. Instead, she ran into Rachel.

"What are you doing here?" Erin blurted when she came around the corner by the home-ec room and saw her best friend holding up a poster. It read, "Go with the luck of the Irish. Go with a winner. Lucille, the new face of CheeseBarkers."

Rachel colored. "I, ah…was looking for you." She

shoved the poster at Madison as if it were on fire. "But then Madison grabbed me and needed some help and…well…I thought it would be okay to help her for a minute." Smiling weakly, she eyed the posters in Erin's hand. "You still have more to put up?"

"Hey, quit dawdling, you guys. We have tons more to do!"

Erin knew that voice. Suze Shillington.

"Your 'luck of the Irish' line is really popular," Suze said, coming up and handing Rachel more posters. "Ratman says it's okay to put these in the bathroom."

Erin stared at her friend. Rachel hadn't just bumped into Madison. She was *helping* with their campaign. She'd even come up with their slogan! Rachel refused to meet her eyes.

Suddenly, Suze seemed to notice Erin. "Oh, hello." She tossed her long, black hair over her shoulder. "Don't let us get in your way."

"I was just leaving," Erin said.

"Wait!" Rachel cried.

But Erin fled.

Erin left school at lunch. She didn't want to see Rachel. Some best friend. Crossing enemy lines like that.

Grabbing her sandwich and an apple, she walked north ten minutes to Seymour Canyon Park. She'd spent many happy hours wandering the trails with Blue. Today, the towering fir trees provided welcome shade from the April sun and gave her a peaceful place to think.

It was one thing for Rachel not to support Blue, but she didn't have to help Lucille win. Things had been different since Rachel had started hanging out with Suze and Madison. She hardly recognized her best friend anymore. Luckily, she and Rachel had no afternoon classes together.

After school, Erin dawdled in the computer lab until most of the kids were gone. Then she grabbed the last of her posters and went around the school, putting them up.

By now, all the good spots were taken. If not by Lucille—pictured running across a field of grass—then by Cupid. The Oresti twins had tacked up a few posters for Patches too. How did Anthony feel about Rachel working for Lucille? Or had Rachel even told him?

Erin was outside the gym hanging up her last poster when she sensed someone behind her. It was Deryk Latham. Wearing his usual black leather jacket and faded old jeans. And videotaping her!

"Hey, you," he said.

That's what he called her this year. *You*. The guy didn't even know her name. Although it was better than last year's "Beast."

"What are you doing?"

He smirked. "What does it look like I'm doing?"

Following her around. Making her life miserable. "Let me guess. Pretending to be the next Steven Spielberg?"

"Spielberg's passé." He aimed the camcorder in Erin's direction. She moved sideways. "My media arts teacher asked me to film the contest. For the school archives." He gestured to the floor. "You dropped something."

Erin looked down. It was a twenty-dollar bill. *Her* twenty-dollar bill, she confirmed after checking her pocket. It must have fallen out when she grabbed the thumb tacks. "Thanks." Surprised, she stooped to retrieve it. She hadn't taken Deryk for the honest type.

"No problem." He repositioned the camcorder. "How about you draw a moustache on Cupid? Or a really ugly bow in Lucille's hair? Shake this contest up a bit?"

That sounded more like the Deryk she knew.

"No way!"

"I need an action shot." He fiddled with a switch on the camcorder. "Could you take your poster down and put it back up again? I need a shot of somebody doing something."

When she didn't move, he looked up. "Please?"

Please? First he told her about the twenty dollars and now he said *please*? Was this really Deryk Latham? Erin turned around and began removing tacks. Whatever. It wouldn't kill her to do what he asked.

"Thanks," he said after she finished. "So, what's Blue's talent going to be?"

"Pardon?" What was he talking about?

"If Blue wins. What's his talent going to be?"

"Talent?" Sometimes Deryk made her feel stupid.

"Haven't you seen the contest rules outside the office? With the sign-up sheet? It's all outlined there," Deryk said.

Erin mumbled her thanks and headed to the office. It had to be a joke. Deryk was bugging her again, like he had last year.

The sign-up sheet was filled with a million names. Half of Carson Heights had signed up to work with the winning dog. And there were the rules beside the sign-up sheet.

The New Face of CheeseBarkers is open to all dogs

nationwide. The winning dog will have its likeness on CheeseBarkers and related products for thirty-six months. Photographs taken of the winning dog will become the lifetime property of the Woofer's Corporation.

Erin skimmed through the details until she came to the last paragraph—the requirements for the winning dog.

The winning dog will be highly photogenic and will allow its face or any part of its body to be reproduced for product sales.

Any part of its body! A lump formed in the back of Erin's throat.

The winning dog will be easygoing and cooperative.

She gulped the lump away. Blue was the easiest-going dog on the planet!

The winning dog will have a skill or talent that can be marketed as part of a media hook.

Erin's heart sank.

This could be a job—seeing, hearing, or search and rescue—or it could be showmanship, agility, retrieving, or other skills. Use of this talent or skill for marketing will be up to the discretion of the Woofer's Corporation.

What about being a good pet? Wasn't that enough? Erin added her name to the bottom of the sign-up sheet. Probably not. Still, there had to be something Blue could do. Some talent or skill he could claim as his own. She just had to figure out what it was.

· ⬭

Rachel was waiting on her front steps when she got home from school. "We need to talk," she said.

"No, we don't." Erin opened the front door. Rachel followed her inside. Blue bounded forward, launching himself into her arms, licking her face, and wagging his tail. She wrapped her arms around his neck and buried her face in his fur. Blue had a skill. Loving her!

"I'm sorry," Rachel said.

Erin ignored her. She walked into the kitchen and let Blue out. When she turned around, Rachel was sitting at the kitchen table. "Let me explain."

"Why you're helping Lucille or why you lied and said you'd help me put up posters?"

Rachel flushed. "Uh…both, I guess."

She didn't want to hear explanations. She just wanted her best friend to support her. And support Blue!

Erin put cheese and crackers on a plate, poured two glasses of lemonade, and then sat down. "Speak."

"First, I didn't lie. I went to school early and I was going to help you, it's just that I ran into Suze and…well…" Guilt was written all over Rachel's face. "She grabbed me and I had a hard time saying no."

Erin snorted. "Yeah, like you had a hard time coming up with that slogan for their posters." She bit into a cracker. It tasted like sawdust.

Rachel fiddled nervously with her lemonade. "You don't understand."

"No, I don't."

"Think about it. My best friend *and* my boyfriend are both trying to get their dog to be the new face of CheeseBarkers. If I get behind you and Blue, Anthony will be upset. If I go with Patches, you'll be upset."

"So you pick neither of us and now we're both upset. That's smart." Erin crushed a piece of cracker under her fingertip. "Not."

"Anthony isn't mad. He understands."

"Yeah, right!"

"He does! He put Patches forward on a dare. He just wants a dog from Carson Heights to win the CheeseBarkers contest. *Any* dog. Think about it! We'd get to appear in a Tawp Dawg video! Maybe even see Caden Vaughan." Rachel's face was awestruck. "Plus, we'd win that money for the dance. We have to nominate the best dog, Erin. It's the only way to make the short list."

"Blue *is* the best dog. And he *can* make the short list." She took a piece of cheese.

"Erin, listen. I'm trying to help you. For this whole entire year you've been trying to get the attention of Zach Cameron, right?"

She nodded.

"And you had it today! You talked to him. He noticed you. He thinks you're a dog whisperer."

He also thought she had a mute friend named Lola.

"If Lucille gets nominated and makes the short list, Zach will need your help readying her for the competition. You'll spend a ton of time together. Zach will get to know you and, before you know it, you'll be going out. It's the perfect plan!"

"I'll get Zach's attention if Blue wins." Plus, Suze's comments about three-legged dogs would stop.

"I told you. Blue's not going to win."

"You don't know that."

"The winning dog needs a talent. Blue doesn't have one." Rachel sipped her lemonade.

"Maybe I should make one up," Erin retorted. "I already have a mute friend that I communicate with by sign language and now I'm a dog whisperer. Maybe

I should give my dog a special imaginary talent too."

"You can't do that."

No, she couldn't. And she wouldn't. "Besides, Blue's already special." She remembered how her mother thought Blue would be the face of animal rights. *That* was Blue's talent! "He can become the face for disabled dogs everywhere."

Rachel grimaced. "Nobody wants to look at a disabled dog on a can of dog food. It's too depressing."

"It's not depressing at all. It shows people that life doesn't stop because of a disability."

Rachel looked skeptical.

"What can Patches do?" Erin demanded. "Or Cupid? Or Lucille?"

"Patches can't do anything." Rachel nibbled at a piece of cheese. "That dog doesn't stand a chance and Anthony knows it. Cupid doesn't stand a chance either, except Miss Pickering says he can do the doggie Salsa." She rolled her eyes.

Erin giggled.

"But Lucille can open the refrigerator, pull out the fruit bin, and remove an apple!" Rachel said. "So Zach's teaching her to open up the fridge, pull out the bin, and remove a package of CheeseBarkers!"

"Huh." Erin buried her face in her lemonade. It was clever, she had to admit that.

"Come on, Erin. Don't be so stubborn. You want to be part of the winning team, don't you? Withdraw Blue."

Erin's head snapped back up. "Is *that* why you came over? To ask me to take Blue out of the competition?"

"No!"

"Good, because I'm not going to."

"Suze just thought it would be better not to split the votes and even Anthony thought—"

Suze Shillington again! Erin stood. "I have a speech to write. You have to leave."

"I didn't mean anything by it, okay? I just thought—"

"I'm not withdrawing Blue." Erin marched down the hall and opened the front door. "This conversation is over."

What about their friendship? Erin wondered as she watched Rachel leave. Was it over too? She shut the door, walked slowly back to the kitchen. She didn't want it to be. She and Rachel had been close since grade two. But she expected loyalty. Especially from her best friend. And she needed Rachel's support right now. But the question was would her friend give it to her?

Chapter Four

THURSDAY morning Erin was determined to have it out with Rachel. If she really *was* trying to help, she should forget Lucille and help get Blue nominated.

The sun warmed Erin's cheeks as she walked past the yellow daffodils blooming in front of the school. It was warm for April. Normally on a day like this, she and Rachel would go to the beach after school. But she couldn't count on Rachel anymore. Lately, she practically had to make an appointment to talk to her.

Entering the school's main door, Erin's gaze was drawn to the bulletin board across the foyer.

"The gimp with the limp."

Someone had taken a big black marker and scrawled the ugly words across Blue's face. Who? Deryk Latham? Is that why he'd nominated Blue? So he could make fun of him?

Erin walked closer. Someone had written on Cupid's poster too. Instead of "I bark for Cheese-

Barkers," it now read, "I barf for CheeseBarkers." Lucille's poster hadn't been touched. And Patches's poster was missing.

Mona Randall appeared beside her. "That really sucks." Mona was tiny; she barely came up to Erin's shoulder.

"No kidding." She and Mona, who was crazy about figure skating, sat beside each other in social studies. Occasionally they ate lunch together. "I wonder how many others have been ruined."

"Four that I've seen." Mona tucked a stray lock of brown hair behind her ear. "If it's any consolation, I think Blue would be great as the new face of CheeseBarkers."

Mona had spent time with Blue in January when she and Erin had done a social studies project on hunger in third-world countries. When she smiled, her blue-green braces glinted in the sunlight. "Why don't you bring him to school tomorrow when they hold the vote? Cupid's here all day. I'm sure they'd let Blue come."

"That's a great idea! I'll ask Mr. Ratzka."

Mona leaned close. "Wait a while. He's on a rant because something else has gone missing from the office. A watch, I think."

"Thanks." Erin watched her friend disappear

down the hall. Mona was sweet. Too bad she and Rachel hadn't hit it off.

Shifting her knapsack, Erin went through the school, checking the other bulletin boards. All her posters had been written on. So had Cupid's. But Patches's posters were missing. Lucille's posters were fine.

Suppressing a sigh, she strode past the home-ec room. Even the smell of baking bread didn't cheer her up. The vote was tomorrow. The posters had to be down by the morning anyway. There wasn't time to replace them.

Erin spun her lock, tossed in her knapsack, dug around for her math book.

"Oh, hey, Erin,"

Erin whirled around to face Suze, Madison, and Rachel. "I was wondering," Suze said, "what you're doing after school?"

Erin blinked. Suze Shillington was asking *her* what she was doing *after school*? Rachel smiled knowingly.

"I...I don't know. Why?"

"I'm having a little pizza thing at my place." Suze touched Erin's arm with claw-like purple nails. Her long, dark hair had a matching purple sheen. "We were hoping you could come."

Suze lived out on Linnet Lane in a huge house overlooking the water. Rachel had been invited to her house a bunch of times this year. Erin hadn't gotten one invite. Until now.

She smiled. "I...ah...sure!" Running Blue in the contest was already getting her invites. When Blue won, she'd be invited everywhere!

"Great!" Suze said.

Rachel beamed. Suze linked her arm through Erin's. "We need strong people on our team, Erin. And you're the best dog trainer at Carson Heights. I know you love Blue, but we need you to work with Lucille." She pouted. "We really want you to withdraw Blue!"

For a minute Erin was flattered. For one thing, it was the longest conversation she'd ever had with Suze. For another, Suze had actually paid her a compliment. She'd called her the best dog trainer at Carson Heights!

But withdraw Blue? No way.

Rachel obviously knew what she was thinking because she gave her a pleading look. "Come on, Erin. It would be great if we could all work together."

Erin hedged. "I don't know." Blue would be perfect for CheeseBarkers. He could win Carson Heights $5,000!

Just then the bell rang. Voices rose around them. Erin was momentarily distracted as people pushed and shoved their way down the hall.

Suze pulled her arm away. "Well, you're either with us or you're not. And today's pizza thing is for Lucille supporters. If you don't withdraw Blue, then I'll withdraw the invitation."

Rachel looked miserable. Madison looked uncomfortable. Erin felt a blush start at the back of her neck. Why did being included hinge on pulling Blue out of the contest? That wasn't fair.

"Why would she withdraw Blue?" Zach asked, coming up behind them.

"Zaaaaach!" Suze practically purred. "Erin's going to withdraw Blue for the same reason Anthony withdrew Patches. Because we all know Lucille is the best dog for the job." Her giggle made Erin want to barf.

"It's not gonna be any fun if dogs keep dropping out," Zach said. "Don't withdraw him, Erin. Unless you think he can't handle it?"

"I—"

"Second bell has gone!" Mr. Ratzka barreled down the hall like a man on a mission. "Move along or you'll have detentions at lunch."

Erin didn't have time for a detention. She had a

speech to give. Because Zach Cameron had spoken. *Don't withdraw him,* he'd said.

And she didn't intend to.

—————————————— •⬭

Erin looked for Rachel at lunch. She wanted to confront her. How could she be friends with someone like Suze? And why wouldn't she support Blue? Even Zach thought he should run.

After twenty minutes of searching, Erin gave up. Rachel had probably taken off with Suze and her gang.

Instead, convinced her speech wasn't *quite* good enough; she went to the library, sat in a quiet cubicle, and rewrote it.

The final product was shorter and better. Now everyone would know Blue was the best choice. She hoped.

The speeches were scheduled for the end of the day. Twenty minutes before the final bell, Erin hurried to the office. Her mouth was dry; her heart was already skipping beats. She hoped to give her speech first and get it over with.

"The school board is demanding these documents as soon as possible," Miss Pickering told Mr. Ratzka as Erin walked through the door. Her desk was covered with papers; she frowned. Cupid, apparently aware of his master's distress, paced restlessly on the brown carpet.

"You can do your speech first," Mr. Ratzka said.

The lines in Miss Pickering's face smoothed out. "That would be wonderful."

Erin sat down. So she'd go second. It wasn't as good as first, but at least it wasn't last.

Zach Cameron appeared carrying cleats and wearing knee pads. Cupid went up, sniffed one of the cleats, snorted, and turned away. Zach chuckled. "I've got soccer practice right after school and I've been late the last two times. Could I go first?"

"Sorry, Zach. You're second," Mr. Ratzka said. He disappeared into the announcer booth.

Great, Erin thought. She was last. Which left her more time to worry. Zach sat down beside her; his arm brushed her sweater. Embarrassed, she eased away.

In the booth, she heard Mr. Ratzka announce the speeches.

Her heart flipped over again. Cupid came up and nudged her foot with his nose.

"*Woof!*"

"Shhh, Cupid. Be quiet!" Miss Pickering flapped her index cards in the dog's face. Thinking it was a game, Cupid lunged for them. "That's my speech!" Miss Pickering pulled the cards back just in time.

When Mr. Ratzka motioned her over, Miss Pickering hurried into the booth, shut the door, and began to speak. "Ladies and gentlemen of Carson Heights, I urge you to choose Cupid as the new face of CheeseBarkers…"

At the mention of his name, Cupid began to whine. And whine. And whine even louder.

Erin snapped her fingers. "Come here, boy," she whispered. "It's okay."

The dog ambled over—his big head low, his tummy even lower.

Zach chuckled under his breath. "Talk about low-riding."

She rubbed Cupid's ears. "He can't help it," she whispered back. "With a stomach that big and legs that short, he doesn't have much choice."

Cupid gazed up at her; a thin line of drool escaped from the side of his mouth.

Erin averted her eyes. She was a dog lover, no question. But in her secret heart-of-hearts, bulldogs were one of her least favorite breeds. It wasn't just their looks either. Their flat noses made them snort. They overate, and they were prone to over-heating. They panted, they gulped in air, and they often had gas!

"So, have you talked to Lola lately?" Zach asked.

Oh man. Not *Lola* again? "Not…not lately." Erin felt a blush flood her face.

In the booth, Erin heard Miss Pickering mention something about how lovable Cupid was. Cupid's ears stood up. He whined again. "Shhhh," Erin and Zach said in unison. They exchanged grins.

Erin was the first to drop her eyes. Here was the perfect opportunity to say something witty and brilliant to Zach Cameron, and she was too terrified to open her mouth. What if he asked her about Lola again?

"I'm glad you didn't drop out," he said.

Erin's head shot up. "You are?" *Could she sound any dumber?*

He nodded. "Blue's cool. Not right for Cheese-Barkers," he added with a smile, "but he's still a great dog."

"Uh, thanks." *Breathe, just breathe.* "Lucille's a great dog too, even if *she* isn't the right choice for CheeseBarkers either."

His smile deepened. "Well, if Blue's not the best choice and Lucille's not the best choice…" His eyes dropped to Cupid. "That just leaves you-know-who."

"*Woooooof!*" Cupid said.

Erin laughed, then held out her fingers to distract the dog. She knew one thing. If Blue had to lose, she'd rather he lost to Lucille than to an ugly, over-weight bulldog. Cupid obviously smelled Erin's ham sandwich on her fingers because he wouldn't stop licking, even when Miss Pickering finished her speech and came out of the booth.

"Cupid, that's enough!" The secretary grabbed the dog's collar and led him back to his blanket under her desk.

Zach stood. "Good luck."

"You too." Erin watched him go into the booth, heard him start by saying, "Hey, friends and fellow Carsonites, go with the luck of the Irish." Listening to Zach made her more nervous, so she pulled out her speech and studied it instead.

A minute later, Cupid moved off his blanket. Slowly he inched his way across the floor on his belly. Miss Pickering was too preoccupied to notice. Erin fought back a laugh and concentrated on her speech.

Thirty seconds later, a quiet whine distracted her. Cupid was at her feet.

Lowering the papers, Erin gazed into two plead-ing brown eyes. The dog whined a second time.

"I don't have anything for you," she whispered.

The third whine was louder and was accompa-nied by a gentle swipe from Cupid's paw.

"Shhhh." She scratched Cupid's head. The dog started licking Erin's hand. He was on the scent of the ham sandwich again. And the more Erin tried to pull away, the more persistent he became. "That's enough! You're getting my speech wet." But Cupid hopped up on his hind legs and almost launched himself into Erin's lap.

"Down, Cupid!" Erin jumped up; her speech fell to the floor. She pushed the dog back, grabbed at her papers.

Cupid grabbed for them too. With his teeth.

She yanked them away. But Cupid wouldn't let go. Growling deep in his throat, he tugged the sheets playfully from side to side.

"Cupid, no!" Her voice rose. "It's not a game!"

Miss Pickering bolted from her chair. "What's going on?"

"Cupid's got my speech."

Reaching down, the secretary pried the dog's teeth apart and removed the papers. They were wet and torn; some of the words were unrecognizable smudges of ink.

"You're up," came a voice from behind.

It was Zach Cameron. He was done. It was Erin's turn now.

Chapter Five

THIS CAN'T BE HAPPENING.

Clutching her ripped speech, Erin walked into the booth. How was she supposed to read it now? She could see a few sentences here and there, but entire passages were gone. Devoured by Cupid's playfulness.

And she'd changed the speech so much at lunch she hadn't had time to memorize it.

"So, please give your attention to our last speaker this afternoon, Erin Morris." Mr. Ratzka gestured her forward.

Erin glanced wildly around the booth, hoping for a miracle. She prayed that someone might rescue her, or a fresh speech might fall from the ceiling, or that she was about to wake up from a bad dream.

But there was no miracle, no fresh speech. This was a walking nightmare, not a bad dream.

She slid onto the stool in front of the mike, smoothed the pages, and cleared her throat.

"Fellow students." Her voice came out in a squeak. Not only was her speech wrecked, but she sounded like a fool. She started over. "Fellow students, I am here today to ask you to choose Mr. Lavender Blue—Blue for short—as the new face of CheeseBarkers."

Her eyes scanned the torn sheets a second time. There had to be something that made sense. Something she could remember to say.

But nothing came to mind. She wanted to run out the door and give up.

But Blue *had* to win. And that thought gave her courage.

She set the sheets aside and began to talk. "My dog, Mr. Lavender Blue, would be perfect as the new face of CheeseBarkers. He is a loving, kind, and loyal pet. He likes people. And people like him."

Well, some people did, at least.

"He has three legs, which you might think of as a disability. But it's not, really. Millions of dogs have disabilities, just like millions of people do. It doesn't mean they are any less valuable."

Erin had warmed up now; her speech might be ruined but she remembered some of it. "People with disabilities are valuable. So are dogs. They can inspire us. They can make us feel that anything is possible. My dog, Mr. Lavender Blue, can be an ambassador for dogs everywhere, those with four legs and those with three."

Erin had planned to say a lot more. But that was all she could remember. She ended with her slogan, "Blue may limp but he's no wimp." Thanking everyone, she handed the microphone back to Mr. Ratzka.

When Erin stepped out of the booth, Miss Pickering was wringing her hands. "My dear, I'm so sorry! Cupid is a bad, bad dog!" She glared at the bulldog, who had taken up his position under her desk. He stared back, his hind end wagging at the mention of his name. "If it's any consolation, you sounded wonderful!"

Erin thanked her, although Miss Pickering was right—it didn't make her feel any better. She looked around the office for Zach but he was gone.

"Well done, Erin," Mr. Ratzka said. "What happened to your speech?" Miss Pickering told him.

He frowned. "You should take Cupid off that diet dog food. He's perpetually hungry."

Miss Pickering sniffed and mumbled something about Cupid being an emotional eater, but Mr. Ratzka wasn't paying attention. "I'm sorry about the speech, Erin, and about the posters." He ran a weary hand over his nearly bald head. "When we find out who defaced them, you can be sure they'll be properly punished."

Erin saw an opportunity. "Mr. Ratzka, may I bring Blue to school tomorrow? My speech was a bust and there's no time to redo the posters. But if the students saw Blue walking around and being normal even with three legs, it might help." She crossed her fingers behind her back. "Cupid is here all the time and the kids know him. It gives him an unfair advantage." It wasn't true. If anything, the only advantage to having Cupid at school was that the kids knew he was a loser.

"Yes," Mr. Ratzka said. "But I would have to let Zach bring Lucille too."

"Of course." Having Lucille at school wasn't perfect, Erin decided as she headed to her locker. But then, few things ever were.

Any hope Erin had of catching Rachel after school was shot down when she saw her friend leave with Suze and her crowd. She called Rachel later that night only to be told Rachel was "out for the evening."

With Suze, no doubt. She could have been with them too. If she'd pulled Blue. That was Suze for you. Calculating and controlling—the kind of girl who attached strings to friendships. Rachel wasn't like that. Or she never used to be.

The next morning, Erin hurried through her shower and breakfast, carefully groomed Blue, and left early for school. Her efficiency paid off: she arrived at school twenty minutes before the first bell.

"Sit, boy." She positioned Blue up against her leg, on the steps by the front entrance. She turned him so his good side was out. The sky was overcast. Sunshine would have given Blue's coat a higher sheen, but he still looked beautiful.

"Nice dog," said a boy from grade nine who stopped to pat his head.

"He's gorgeous." His friend scratched Blue's chin.

Erin smiled. "I think so." Reminding them of today's vote, she asked them to support Blue.

They were noncommittal, but at least they'd stopped to pat Blue.

And that didn't happen again for almost ten minutes. For ten *embarrassing* minutes as Erin endured people looking at Blue and then quickly looking away. Or worse, looking at Blue, laughing, and then looking away.

"You brought him!" Mona leaned down and ruffled Blue's ears. "Hello, Blue. How's it going?" The dog responded with a sloppy kiss across Mona's cheek. Both girls giggled.

"Sit down," Erin urged. "Keep me company."

"I can't."

Erin couldn't hide her disappointment.

"Sorry. Miss Rutherford gave me an extension on my history paper and she won't dock my mark as long as I get it to her before first bell." Mona scratched Blue behind his ear as she turned to go. "Don't worry though, Blue has my vote."

Mine too, Erin thought, glancing down the sidewalk. Catching sight of Rachel and Anthony, she waved them over.

"Hey!" Rachel gave her an uneasy smile. "How's it going?" Excited to see Rachel, Blue whined and tugged on his leash.

"Okay...I guess." Erin loosened Blue. He lunged playfully at Rachel, smothering her with kisses.

Rachel laughed and leaned down to give him a hug. She'd always loved Blue. At least *that* hadn't changed.

"We need to talk," Erin said.

Anthony glanced uneasily from Erin to Rachel. "I gotta go." He pecked Rachel on the cheek, then bolted up the stairs.

Rachel rolled her eyes and sat beside Erin. "Men. The *talk* word scares them every time."

Erin didn't even smile. Instead she asked, "Rachel, what's going on? I thought we were friends."

"We are, silly." Rachel leaned down and fiddled with Blue's collar. "I don't know what you're talking about."

"Yes, you do."

Sighing, Rachel dropped Blue's collar and looked up. "Just because we disagree doesn't mean we aren't friends." She tossed her long blonde hair over her shoulder. "I love Blue, but he's not going to be the new face of CheeseBarkers. And the sooner you get that through your head, the better."

"He'd have a chance if he had my *friends* behind him." Erin said hotly. "Besides, if you thought about it, you'd see that he's the right choice. Instead you're being brainwashed by Suze Shillington. And the only reason she wants Lucille to win is because she's after Zach!"

"Lucille is the best choice," Rachel said. "Even Anthony agrees."

A lump formed in Erin's throat. "I thought friends were supposed to support each other."

"I thought friends weren't supposed to make each other feel guilty!" Rachel challenged. "You're just jealous that I'm spending so much time with Suze."

"That's not true." Erin felt a flush creep into her cheeks.

Rachel didn't miss the telltale color. "You're a lousy liar. It is *so* true." When Erin was silent, she continued. "If you weren't so stubborn and you did what I suggested once in a while—like flirt with Zach and support Lucille—this wouldn't be happening." She grabbed her bag and stood. "You'd be part of the in crowd, one of *us*."

Erin watched her walk away. Rachel *was* attaching strings to their friendship. Just like Suze Shillington. How could she stay friends with her and remain true to herself? There had to be a way. She simply had to find it.

—————————— • ◯

The day dragged. Looking after Blue pushed the problem with Rachel to the back of her mind. Though he was unnerved by the students rushing through the halls, once Blue got to class he settled quietly. At lunch, when she went to the gym to vote, everyone talked about how well-behaved he was, and how friendly. It left Erin more hopeful than ever. At the end of the day when they returned to homeroom to hear the results of the vote, she felt almost confident.

Almost.

"Take your seats, people," Miss Thibault yelled over the laughter and loud voices. "The announcement will be made shortly."

Three minutes until the bell and the students in Erin Morris's homeroom were already in weekend mode. The Oresti twins played hacky sack in the corner. Deryk Latham arm wrestled with Peter McNab. Mona was telling a group of girls about her upcoming skating competition.

Erin was quiet. Reaching down to scratch Blue, she wondered how Zach Cameron was feeling. Was he nervous too? Probably not. People like Zach didn't get nervous. For once, she was glad they didn't have any classes together. She couldn't stand the thought of being in the same room with him when the results were announced.

How would he feel if she won and he lost?

Worse, how would *she* feel if he won and she lost?

"Good afternoon, students and staff. Just before we break for the weekend, I would like to announce who will represent Carson Heights in the CheeseBarkers competition." At the sound of Mr. Ratzka's voice over the PA system, the noise in the classroom faded. There was a quiet shuffling as people took their seats. Erin dug her fingers into Blue's thick fur.

"The dog that will go forward to compete in the

CheeseBarkers competition," Mr. Ratzka said, "is our very own Cupid, who received 312 votes."

There was stunned silence, followed by a few muffled groans.

Cupid? No way.

It should have been Blue.

Erin sensed heads swiveling in her direction. Eyes studying her. Struggling to keep her face blank, she stared straight ahead. In a perfect world, it would have been Blue. In a less than perfect world, it would have been Lucille. Lucille was beautiful. Lucille could open the fridge.

Cupid was ugly and he ate everything in sight.

Including her speech!

"The runner-up was Lucille with 290 votes. And Blue with five votes."

Five votes.

Oh God. More eyes sought her out. She wanted to disappear. Only *five*?

"Just a reminder that there is a meeting tomorrow morning for those people who signed up to make the video. Please meet in the band room at 10:00 a.m. and help us make Cupid the new face of CheeseBarkers. Have a good weekend, everyone."

Chairs pushed back, books slammed down, voices rose in disgust.

"Can you believe it?"

"The corpulent Cupid…did you vote for him?"

"Not on your life, man."

"I'm not working with Cupid. I'm outta there."

Bodies weighted with knapsacks crowded the aisles. Erin stroked Blue's fur and played with his collar, pretending it needed to be straightened. He wagged his tail and gazed adoringly at her, his brown eyes full of love. He didn't care about losing. Not in the least.

Erin did. But she had to pretend otherwise. At least until she got home. She pulled out Blue's leash, fastened it to his collar.

Rachel was one aisle over. When Erin caught her eye, she shrugged and looked away. Anthony wouldn't even look at her.

"I'm sorry Blue didn't win, Erin." It was Mona.

Erin fell into step beside her. "Me too."

"Cupid's a total disaster."

"I know." Cupid might be trainable. If they had a year. Or three. But they had just ten days. There was no way they could do anything that fast.

"Look on the bright side." Mona's blue-green braces glinted when she grinned. "Blue lost, but you saved him from the wrath of Deryk Latham."

Erin frowned. "What do you mean?"

"Didn't you hear?" They walked out of the classroom and into the hall. "Deryk Latham is producing the video we send to CheeseBarkers."

Deryk was doing the video? The meanest guy in the whole school? Okay, so he *had* returned her twenty dollars. That still didn't make him totally nice.

"I'd quit the training committee if I were you," Mona said. "Cupid will never make the finals, no matter how good the video is. Why waste your time?"

Quit the committee? Erin stopped in front of her locker. Should she?

"I've gotta go," Mona said. "Have a good weekend." She disappeared down the hall.

Erin opened her locker and gathered her homework. Blue paced impatiently behind her. A couple of people stopped to pat him. Once person offered Erin a sympathetic smile and said it was too bad he'd lost.

It was too bad all right. She slammed her locker shut and hurried out of the school. Too bad the students hadn't picked a winner like Blue instead of a loser like Cupid.

That left Erin with a decision to make. Should she go to tomorrow's meeting and do everything she could to make Cupid look good on the video? Or should she quit the committee like Mona suggested?

She had the rest of the night to decide.

Chapter Six

ERIN CRADLED THE COCKER SPANIEL'S HEAD, stared into its big brown eyes, and tried not to breathe deeply. The antiseptic smell in the examining room always left her queasy.

"It's okay, sweet thing. Soon it'll be over."

The animal was the most recent stray to arrive at the SPCA. Judging by the way it cowered when anyone came close, Erin suspected it had been mistreated.

Richard positioned the needle above the dog's hip. "Now," he murmured. Erin tightened her hold. The dog yelped and howled; its nails skittered as it tried to run across the steel examining table.

Afterward, Erin offered the spaniel half a biscuit. The dog crunched it quickly and nosed around for more. "That's it!" She scratched the dog behind her curly, blonde ears.

"She's taken to you." Richard threw the needle away and peeled off his latex gloves. "No surprise. You're the biggest dog magnet I've ever seen."

"I wish I could adopt them all, but I'd never convince my parents." She eyed the clock on the wall. Only fifteen minutes till closing.

"How about we brush her again?" Richard suggested.

"Okay." Last week's attempt had been a disaster, but the dog trusted her more now.

"You settle her out front and I'll bring the brush."

Erin let the spaniel walk around the waiting room while she gathered up her algebra books, shut down the computer, and switched the phone to automatic answer.

"How's the algebra coming?" Richard asked when he came out and saw Erin's books on the counter.

"Not great. I'm getting by, but barely." Algebra was the last thing she wanted to think about. She lifted the dog onto her knee and stroked her neck. "I think we should call her Peaches. She's sweet and she's got streaks of apricot in her fur."

Richard crouched down beside them. "Keep talking and petting her," he suggested quietly. "Another minute or so, I'll touch her lightly with the brush."

"Blue lost today," Erin said softly. Richard removed the brush from his back pocket. "He only got five votes. Cupid won instead." She'd given

Richard a few details about the contest when she'd phoned earlier in the week and asked to change her shift to Friday night.

"That's too bad." Richard touched Peaches with the brush. The dog squirmed.

"I signed up to help but I've decided to pull out."

The dog tried to twist free, but, as Erin talked, the squirming lessened. "Lots of people signed up so I won't be missed. Besides, I couldn't train Cupid." Mona was right: *nobody* could train Cupid. "It would have been different if Blue had been picked." *Five* votes. She still couldn't believe it.

"I'm not sorry Blue lost." Richard moved the brush from Peaches's haunches to her back. "I wouldn't want to see his face on a package of dog food."

"Why not?"

Richard eased the brush toward Peaches's neck. "The contest is animal exploitation."

Peaches tried to get out from under the brush but Erin soothed her. "What do you mean?"

"Do you know how much the Woofer's Corporation makes on its food?" Erin shook her head. "Millions probably. To them $5,000 is pocket change. So they hold a contest, open it to school kids with dogs, and they look like heroes. In reality, they're saving money—they have a dog that's not in a union so they can work him as long and as hard as they want."

Erin hadn't thought of that. But it didn't surprise her that Richard had. He was a licensed veterinarian and passionate about animal rights. "Well, it doesn't matter," Erin said, "because Carson Heights won't be sending a dog to the finals anyway."

"But other dogs will be going, and I shudder to think how they'll be treated."

Now she understood why Richard hadn't been happy with her requesting Saturday off. He didn't think she should be involved in the contest in the first place.

When Richard lowered the brush to Peaches's stomach, the dog began to writhe and whine. "That's enough for tonight." He put the brush aside and began gathering up the loose fur.

Erin gave Peaches one last cuddle before putting her on the floor.

"You're doing well with her," Richard said. "Anne noticed."

Erin's heart skipped a beat. Anne was the SPCA manager. She decided who stayed in the volunteer positions and who got paid for working at the SPCA.

"She also noticed that you've been taking on extra shifts without being asked."

"I like working here." She brushed fur from her jeans. "I'd like a paying position."

"Not yet." Richard's hazel eyes softened at the look of disappointment on Erin's face. "But soon," he added. "Anne wants to schedule you for an extra shift one night a week. If you can handle that plus your regular Saturday shift, she'll bump you to a paying position after six months."

Six months. Next October. She'd be in grade nine and she'd have a real job. With money to spend!

She grinned. "It's a deal!"

"Just make sure your algebra mark doesn't slip," Richard cautioned as Erin coaxed Peaches through the door to the kennels out back. "Otherwise your parents will have my head."

Erin had planned to skip Saturday's training meeting. But Rachel had called while she was at the SPCA and left a message that she'd see her there. Erin decided it was only fair to show up and tell them she couldn't get involved. Besides, if she went to the meeting, she could talk to Rachel about Suze.

The band room was almost empty the next morning. The drum sets and music stands had been pushed into the corner, and hardly anybody had shown up. Nobody wanted to work with Cupid.

Then Erin noticed Suze Shillington.

She sat on a chair near Mrs. Abernathy's desk, tossing her straight black hair and laughing that stupid, high-pitched laugh of hers. Rachel, Anthony, Joseph, Madison, and Zach surrounded her.

What was *she* doing here?

Chasing after Zach like a lovesick puppy.

So much for talking to Rachel. She wouldn't even try with Suze around. Suppressing a sigh, Erin hung her coat and headed for the doughnut table, where she helped herself to an apple fritter and nodded hello to Deryk Latham.

"Erin! Thank goodness you made it." It was Miss Pickering. Still smelling of lavender and wearing her hair in a braid. But instead of her usual skirt and blazer she wore a neon pink sweatshirt, baggy black pants, and lime green running shoes. "We had more than thirty people on the sign-up sheet. Less than half have shown up."

What would Miss Pickering think when she quit too? Mumbling something about commitments, she bit into her apple fritter.

"It's a good thing Cupid has you on his side, Erin. Everybody knows how good you are with dogs. If anybody can train Cupid well enough to win that $5,000, it's you."

No way. "I don't think so." The bulldog sniffed under the table for crumbs. The dog needed a face transplant, a personality switch, probably doggie counseling too. Training him was a job for professionals.

"It's true. I heard Zach Cameron tell his buddies that the other day."

"He did?" Zach Cameron had talked to his *buddies* about her?

Miss Pickering nodded. "He most certainly did. I'm so glad you're not letting Carson Heights down, Erin." She picked up the tray of doughnuts and moved away.

Great. Like, no pressure. Listlessly, she picked at a raisin in her fritter.

At the front of the room, Mr. Ratzka called for attention.

"Thank you for coming," Mr. Ratzka said. "I appreciate you giving up your Saturday morning." He cleared his throat. "No matter who you voted for, the fact is, Cupid won fairly. And we must all get behind him." Erin's eyes sought out Rachel, but the group around Mrs. Abernathy's desk was too preoccupied selecting doughnuts to look up. And laughing as Cupid danced up on his hind legs to grab at crumbs.

"Two other things," Mr. Ratzka continued. "Please don't leave today until we have a group photo taken for the *Carson Heights Crier*." The *Crier* was the school newspaper. Erin had noticed the school photographer, Nicola Scott, hovering by the doughnuts.

"Second, it's important that you honor your commitment to Cupid. We need to work fast. Be prepared to give up time after school and on the weekends. If it's a problem, see Zach Cameron or myself before leaving today. We need to know who we can count on."

They couldn't count on her. Her parents had come down hard about her second shift at the SPCA. They were concerned that she was taking on too much, and that her algebra mark was suffering. They'd given her an ultimatum: if she didn't get her algebra mark up, she had to quit the SPCA. And there was no way she was doing that. She couldn't work with Cupid. She didn't have time. She'd tell Mr. Ratzka after the meeting.

"And now," Mr. Ratzka said, "let me turn things over to Zach Cameron."

Zach appeared beside him. Even in jeans and a plain white T-shirt, the guy looked hot. Someone said he lifted weights. By the size of his shoulders, Erin believed it.

"Thank you, Mr. Ratzka. Today we have to figure out how to film Cupid and make him look good." A wave of laughter broke out. Zach grinned good-naturedly. "We have to figure out his talent so he can get short-listed and go on to win the $5,000 grand prize. And the video has to be submitted in nine days."

"I think we should get Cupid to open the fridge and take out dog food the way Lucille does." Suze batted her huge, dark eyelashes at Zach. How did she move them with all that mascara on? Erin wondered.

"We don't have time. It took me months to train Lucille to do that," Zach said.

"Cupid loves food," someone yelled. "It wouldn't be that hard."

Maybe not. But who wanted to watch a video of Cupid from behind? Erin glanced around the room. The term *butt-ugly* had been coined with him in mind. Where was he anyway?

"Let's teach him to do a high-five," another person said.

"Or juggle," one of the Oresti twins suggested. Laughter rippled through the group.

"He does a lovely Salsa." Miss Pickering held up a CD. "I brought his special music."

Mr. Ratzka turned on the portable CD player. "It's cut number four," Miss Pickering said. "Salsa Fever." As Mr. Ratzka searched, she called Cupid. "Come here, boy. It's time to dance."

The Oresti twins snorted. Deryk Latham snickered. Erin smiled to herself. Who'd ever heard of a bulldog doing the Salsa?

Miss Pickering gazed around the room. "Where's Cupid?" A worried frown puckered her forehead. "Where did he go?"

People began looking under the food table, between chairs, behind the stage.

Cupid had disappeared.

"It's not like him to leave with doughnuts still around." A note of panic crept into Miss Pickering's voice.

"He probably wandered down the hall." Zach pointed. The band room door was wide open.

The students fanned out. Within minutes, Cupid was found outside the home-ec room.

"They cooked Chinese food yesterday," Miss Pickering said when she returned with him. "And chow mein is your favorite, isn't it, Cupid?"

Cupid blinked up at his owner. A thin line of drool escaped down his chin. *Yuk*, Erin thought. The dog salivated at the slightest mention of food.

Miss Pickering took Cupid to the open area at the side of the room. She put the dog down and nodded at Mr. Ratzka. The music began.

It was up-tempo and fast, with a South American rhythm Erin loved.

Miss Pickering tapped left, rocked back, swung forward. At first, Cupid sat there, his head cocked to one side, watching her. But when Miss Pickering snapped her fingers, Cupid jumped to attention. He pranced right, left, forward, back—always following Miss Pickering's lead. And when Miss Pickering picked up the pace, Cupid did too.

Erin couldn't believe it. He looked like a bow-legged clown with his short legs and that silly bull-dog grin on his face. And he had a crazy sense of timing that was off. But he was fun to watch.

As the music reached a crescendo, Miss Pickering raised her hands in the air and clapped three times. Cupid jumped and spun. Then, just as the music hit its final note, he collapsed on the floor in a dead dog pose.

Erin laughed and clapped with everyone else. The dog had a sense of the dramatic too.

"Well?" Miss Pickering asked. Her face was flushed; a sheen of perspiration covered her fore-head. "What do you think?"

"That was great," Zach said.

"You'll have to find someone else to do the rou-tine with him, though." She sank gratefully into a chair Mr. Ratzka brought over for her. "I'm not doing that for the video. No way."

"How many people think we should get Cupid to do a dance routine?" Zach asked. "How about a show of hands."

Erin raised her hand along with everybody else in the room. Obviously Cupid was trainable. Not to that piece of music, though. He looked cute but his short legs couldn't keep up to the beat. Still, if he knew how to jump and spin, he could learn a few other moves. Too bad there wasn't more time to train him.

"I'll learn the routine and work with Cupid," Suze offered.

Erin blinked. Suze?

"I studied ballet for five years," she said. "I'm good at choreography."

But Suze *hated* Cupid.

"And I'm very photogenic." Suze tilted her chin, smiled self-consciously.

So that was it. Suze wanted *her* fifteen minutes of fame. She wanted to be in the CheeseBarkers video.

Beside her, someone made a soft puking noise. It was Deryk Latham.

"It's a lovely offer, Suzanne, but you don't have much experience with dogs," Miss Pickering said. "Cupid can be a handful and I'm not sure the two of you would be the best pair."

"I nominate Erin Morris," Rachel said.

What?

Rachel stared across the room at her; Erin shook her head. *No, no, no!*

Suze frowned, leaned over, and whispered something in Rachel's ear. Rachel shook her head and whispered something back. Then she said, "Erin is experienced. If anyone can make Cupid look good, she can."

Erin knew Rachel was trying to do her a favor. Make things right by getting her an important job. But she didn't have the time and she didn't want the responsibility.

"Rachel's right," Zach said. "Erin would be the best person to work with Cupid."

The best person to work with Cupid. Zach's words sent a ripple of excitement through her. Zach thought she would be *the best.* Suze glared. The thrill dissolved. It didn't matter anyway. She couldn't do the job. "I...I can't."

"Why not?" Zach asked.

Because my algebra mark sucks and if I don't improve it, I'll have to quit the SPCA and I won't do that for a stupid bulldog named Cupid. "Because... because I have a work conflict."

Suze looked like she'd won the lottery. "I guess I'm it," she said smugly.

"What kind of a conflict?" Zach asked.

Erin hesitated. Her job at the SPCA was a volunteer position. Deryk Latham teased her all the time because it didn't pay. But it was a commitment she had to honor. Besides, it was the only excuse she had. She wouldn't tell them about her algebra mark. "I've been asked to take on an extra shift at the SPCA. And I can't get any more Saturdays off."

"I can't come Saturday either," Deryk Latham said. "I have archery classes."

Archery? Who practiced archery?

"But I can meet Sunday if she can meet then," he added.

She? So now she was *she* instead of *you?*

"I don't have time," Erin said. "Cupid's rhythm is off. He probably needs new music. For sure, he needs someone who can work with him every day."

"We'll help you," several voices cried out.

"That's right," Zach said. "You'd be doing the final routine with Cupid, but you wouldn't have to train alone. You'd have help."

They didn't get it. Dogs couldn't take direction from a bunch of people. It was too confusing. It didn't matter anyway. She didn't *want* to do it.

"I don't have time," she said again.

"Come on, don't let us down," someone yelled.

"We need you."

"Yeah, come on, Erin. Zach's right; you're the best." This from Zach's friend, Steve.

You're the best. We need you. After months of being ignored and overlooked, the words went straight to Erin's head. But seconds later, sanity returned. She really *didn't* have time to train Cupid.

"So what if we meet all day Sunday and three or four days after school, depending on Erin's availability?" Zach suggested.

"Works for me," Deryk said. "As long as it works for her."

Erin was struck speechless. Why couldn't Deryk Latham just shut up?

"Then I nominate Erin again," Rachel said.

Rachel too. Why couldn't *everybody* just shut up?

"I second it," Miss Pickering added.

She was being railroaded! She *had* to say something.

"But I...I—"

Zach interrupted her a second time. "How about a show of hands?"

Every single hand in the room went up, except for Erin's and Suze Shillington's.

"Then it's settled," Zach said.

"What about me?" Suze Shillington pouted. "What can I do?"

Up on stage, Zach looked like a trapped animal. He glanced from Suze to Erin and back to Suze again.

Erin seized the opportunity. "Suze can train Cupid," she yelled out. "I really don't mind."

Rachel leaned over and whispered something to Suze. The other girl stared at Erin with an unreadable expression in her eyes.

"We'll find something else for you to do," Zach promised Suze. "Maybe you can help with the final edit on the video."

As Zach talked about their next meeting, Erin fumed. She had to get out of it. She had two shifts at the SPCA now, plus the strings program, plus she had to maintain her algebra mark. Plus she did *not* want to train an overweight, drooling bulldog!

The group photo took far too long because Cupid refused to stand still. Everyone laughed; Erin barely cracked a smile. She felt Rachel staring and Suze glaring at her, but she wouldn't meet their eyes. Afterward, when Rachel approached her, Erin turned away and headed for the coat rack. She was so angry, she didn't trust herself to speak.

"Hey, thanks a million." Zach dropped his arm on her shoulder.

Erin thought she would faint.

"I really appreciate you taking this on." He gave her a squeeze.

His arm was, like, practically *around* her; his muscles were *mountainous*.

She was going to die. Right here. This minute.

"Don't worry about your schedule." He kept his arm in place and steered her toward the coats. "We'll work around it."

What schedule? What SPCA? What algebra? All Erin could think about was this: *they fit*.

Zach's arm fit perfectly on her shoulder, his hip bumped perfectly against hers, he was the perfect height. They *fit*.

Just as she'd always dreamed they would.

"I have—" Her tongue twisted. She could barely breathe. *I have to quit, but I can't with you standing this close and smelling this good.* He smelled like limes…or maybe a summer morning. "I…um…nine days isn't enough time to train Cupid and do the video. I…um…have some concerns." One of them was Suze Shillington. She was sending Erin murderous looks from across the room.

"Don't worry. You won't be alone."

She wouldn't be alone.

Zach gave her shoulders a final squeeze before

dropping his arm and grabbing his coat. "Together we'll manage."

Together we'll manage.

"Besides, there's always the magic of editing." He winked at her and then glanced at Deryk Latham, who had joined them. "We can make anything look good, right, Latham?"

Deryk's pale blue eyes narrowed; his lip curled. "Fake it till you make it. Isn't that your saying, Cameron?"

"Whatever."

The two of them eyed each other. The silence grew uncomfortable, until Deryk moved away. Zach stared at his retreating back. Judging by the look on his face, Erin could tell he didn't have the warm fuzzies for Deryk Latham either.

Great. Not only did she have to juggle school, the SPCA, and Cupid, but it looked like she had to keep Deryk and Zach from killing each other too.

Why wasn't life easy?

Chapter Seven

CRIN PUT HER SANDWICH down and grabbed the milk from the fridge. She should have said no to Zach Cameron.

"It's not the end of the world," her mother said again.

Maybe not, but it was the end of her dream—her dream of winning Carson Heights $5,000. Blue could have won. Cupid didn't stand a chance. She poured herself a glass of milk, sat back down. Blue was on the mat under the sink. His big brown eyes studied her. He was so gorgeous.

Unlike certain bulldogs she knew.

"You said yourself that Cupid knows how to dance. That he's used to music. It shouldn't be that hard to teach him a few extra moves."

"I don't want to teach him a few extra moves. I don't want to teach him *any* moves."

You won't be alone. Together we'll manage. Had Zach Cameron really said those things to her?

He really had.

He'd put his arm around her too. And that's when she'd been struck dumb. She'd lost her tongue and her mind at the very same time. She bit into her ham sandwich. It was tasteless.

"Besides, it's a lot of work. And you and Dad were freaking over me taking an extra shift at the SPCA."

"We weren't *freaking*." Her mother smiled. "But schoolwork is a priority. If your algebra mark slips any lower, you'll definitely have to cut back on your extracurricular activities."

Her parents had high standards when it came to schoolwork. It had never been a problem before. Until this year. And algebra.

"Rachel shouldn't have nominated you without your permission." Mom picked at her salad. "You need to talk to her about that."

She needed to talk to Rachel about a lot of things.

"She has a strong personality," her mother reminded her. "She takes advantage of the fact that you're easygoing. You have to stand up for yourself. And learn to say no once in a while."

Mom was right. If Zach hadn't come along the other day, would the girls have talked her into pulling Blue? Erin liked to think not, but she didn't know for sure. She had a hard time resisting the pull of the popular kids. If only Rachel hadn't opened her big, fat mouth.

Rachel called a few minutes later. She had to babysit her little brother, but would Erin come over and keep her company?

What's the matter? Erin wanted to ask. *Is Suze busy?* Instead, she said she'd be over in a while.

"I thought you'd never get here," Rachel said when Erin knocked on her door an hour later.

Erin stepped into the Hydes' cluttered hallway. "I had stuff to do." Hooks on the right side of the wall held coats and hats and umbrellas; a long bench on the left was piled with books and tennis racquets.

"He's driving me crazy!" Rachel gestured into the living room where Keegan was playing cars on his plastic race track. Seeing Erin, he launched himself across the room and into her arms. "Erin! Wanna play?"

"He has a cold," Rachel warned. "Don't get too close."

Giggling, Erin ruffled the little boy's hair. "Maybe later, okay?"

"Want a soda?" Rachel asked.

"Sure."

After retrieving drinks, they curled up on a navy

sectional in the family room. "Why wouldn't you talk to me after the meeting?" Rachel asked. "What's your problem anyway?"

"Let me think." Erin paused. "Maybe because you tried to get me to pull Blue? Or because Suze invited me to her place and then uninvited me? Or wait. Maybe it's the fact that you nominated me to train a stupid, overweight bulldog."

"I did you a favor," Rachel said. "The least you can do is thank me."

"I'm not thanking you. You've complicated my life."

"I have not." Rachel dug into the bowl of chips on the coffee table. "Zach will get to know you better now. Although maybe you don't need my help. I saw him put his arm around you this morning," she added slyly.

Blushing, Erin took a chip and scooped up some dip. "Zach could have gotten to know me better if Blue had won too."

"Like *that* was going to happen. You want him to ask you out and this is perfect."

She did want Zach to ask her out. As long as he didn't ask her about Lola at the same time!

"You've been hiding out at the SPCA all winter," Rachel continued. "You need to get out more. When people get to know you, they'll love you as much as I do."

Suze would never love her. Especially now that Rachel had nominated her to be in the video. "Why do you guys care about Cupid all of a sudden anyway? You wanted Lucille to win."

Rachel sipped her drink. "Like Ratzka said, Cupid was picked so we need to get behind him." When Erin gave her a skeptical look, Rachel admitted, "Okay. Suze wanted to get involved because she knew Zach would be."

Erin figured as much. "I don't know what you see in her. She's mean."

"She's not. You need to get to know her, that's all."

Rachel was a positive thinker. She saw the good in everybody. But in this case, Rachel was wrong.

"Suze really wanted to do that video," Rachel added. "You don't know how hard it was convincing her that you were the right choice."

Oh, she could imagine. She remembered that murderous glare. Erin grabbed more chips. "Cupid's never gonna win. He's ugly."

"You told me once there was no such thing as an ugly dog."

"I lied."

Rachel grinned. "You never lie."

Except about Lola. "So I made a mistake. Cupid is ugly. The ugliest. He can dance but not well enough to make the finals." She licked salt from her fingers.

"Nobody expects him to make the finals. That's why it's so perfect." Rachel sipped her soda. "You show up and train Cupid. You get to know everybody, everybody gets to know you. They see what a great person you are. *Zach* sees what a great person you are. The video gets made, Cupid loses, but you end up part of our group."

"No way. Cupid loses and everybody *blames* me."

"They can't blame you for a pathetic bulldog. I won't let them."

There was Rachel's optimistic nature again.

"You're willing to work with Blue even though he's handicapped," Rachel added. "I don't know why you won't work with a handicapped bulldog."

"Cupid's not handicapped."

"With a face like that?" Rachel asked. "Are you nuts? Of course he's handicapped."

They burst out laughing.

"Besides," Rachel said after a minute, "Cupid looked pretty cute doing the Salsa. With you training him, he just *might* make the finals. Stranger things have happened."

They could see it now. Mr. Ratzka would make the announcement. Our very own Cupid has made the finals in the CheeseBarkers competition. And it's all because of the talented Erin Morris. Kids would come up to her in the halls, invite her out for pizza, to parties. She'd be the most—

"Erin." Rachel tapped her knee, pointed to her hand. She was trying to dip her chip into a bowl of rose potpourri instead of dip. "If you want to get Cupid to the finals, you're gonna have to stop daydreaming so you can train him."

The rest of the weekend went by in a flurry of chores and homework, walks with Blue, and a marathon of card games with her dad. Every once in a while, Erin would think of Cupid and worry.

Training him was a big responsibility. What if she couldn't do it? And how would she handle her homework, the SPCA, the strings program? She would juggle. Because Rachel was right. Nobody expected Cupid to win. And it was a great way for her to get to know people. For Zach to get to know her.

Monday morning was cool and rainy. Erin got

soaked walking to school. By the time she got to her locker, however, she didn't care about her wet jeans. Six people said hello to her in about two minutes. *Six*. Including Zach's best friend, Steve, and Becky Goldman, a popular girl in grade nine, She hadn't even started training Cupid yet, and already it was paying off.

"Just a few announcements this morning." Mr. Ratzka's voice boomed out of the PA system. Erin whispered a hello to Mona and took her seat. Across the room, Rachel waved. Erin waved back.

"We've had another theft," Mr. Ratzka said. "This one from the band room."

The whispering in the classroom stopped. Even the Oresti twins stopped arm wrestling.

"Sometime between Friday afternoon and Monday morning, a silver bracelet went missing from Mrs. Abernathy's desk."

Suze had sat near the desk on Saturday. So had Rachel and a few others. Had one of them taken the bracelet? Erin glanced across the room. Rachel tapped a pencil against her desk. She looked bored, not guilty. Besides, she might be a lot of things, but she wasn't a thief.

"In a little over a week, we've had a set of keys, a watch, and now this bracelet stolen," Mr. Ratzka said. "I would like the person responsible to return these items to the office as soon as possible." After reminding them that Carson Heights was a great school and that he was sure the theft was the act of one seriously misguided individual, Mr. Ratzka wished them all a good morning.

"Somebody told me it was worth $1,000," Mona said as they walked out together. "Why would Mrs. Abernathy leave a bracelet like that in a desk drawer?"

"Who knows." Erin rubbed at her eye.

Mona peered at her. "What's wrong?"

"My eye has been watering since I got to school. I must have a hair in it. Or a piece of dirt."

"Let me look." Mona couldn't see anything.

"I'll go and wash it out," Erin said. "Could you tell Ms. Carter that I'll be late for algebra?"

"Sure."

Erin ducked into the washroom just in time to hear a familiar voice float out from one of the stalls. "Thank God you saved me from humiliating myself with Cupid." It was Suze Shillington.

From behind the closed door of the second stall came another familiar voice. "You're welcome." It was Rachel.

Erin's blood stopped. It couldn't be.

"Let Erin Morris make a fool of herself," Suze continued. "I don't need to."

A cold chill raced down Erin's spine. They *were* talking about her.

"What has she got to lose?" Suze asked with a laugh. "Not many friends, that's for sure."

Rachel's reply was drowned out by the sound of a flushing toilet.

The stall doors opened simultaneously. Rachel stepped out of one; Suze stepped out of the other.

"Oh, hello." Suze met Erin's eyes with an embarrassed laugh. "We were just talking about you."

"I heard."

Rachel's face was plum red. "Erin, look, it's not what you think, I—"

But Erin had heard enough. She bolted out the door. And by the time she got to algebra, both eyes were watering. Allergies, she told Ms. Carter. That's all it was. She was highly allergic to Suze Shillington. And she was starting to be allergic to Rachel Hyde too.

Chapter Eight

THE DAY WENT FROM BAD TO WORSE. When Ms. Carter handed back their algebra homework, Erin had gotten three-quarters of the answers wrong. How would she pass Friday's test?

Then she caught her favorite pink sweater on her locker door and tore a huge hole right in the middle. Just what she needed, Erin fumed as she headed down the hall to the multi-purpose room for Cupid's first training session. Something else for Suze to tease her about.

Suze's words played through her mind. *Let Erin Morris make a fool of herself. She has no friends anyway.*

Had Rachel lied the other day when she'd said training Cupid was the perfect plan? Had she nominated her just to save Suze from being humiliated? Had they dreamed the idea up together?

The thought made her sick to her stomach.

Erin heard laughter as she turned the corner. She

stopped in the doorway just in time to see Cupid tear past with something clutched between his teeth. "What's going on?"

Deryk stopped laughing long enough to say, "Cupid's having a snack." Steve and Jason were laughing too hard to speak. Even Nicola and Raelene were giggling.

Cupid dropped his prize in the corner and licked it.

"What is it?" Erin asked.

"A croissant, we think. But we're not sure."

"Mr. Ponchet had his French class in here again today and they had a pile of food," Steve added.

The roof had been leaking in Mr. Ponchet's class, so he'd been teaching French in the multi-purpose room. When Erin had explained that the carpeted, open area was perfect for refining Cupid's dance routine, Mr. Ponchet agreed to let them use the room at lunch and after school.

After finishing his snack and giving the carpet a few more licks, Cupid pranced back to Jason. "You still hungry, boy?" Jason held something in his finger. It looked like a piece of cheese.

Cupid barked.

Jason jiggled his finger. Cupid jumped into the air, grabbed the food, and tore off again.

"All that food's not good for him," Erin said.

"Oh, lighten up." Annoyance flicked across his face. "It's just a piece of Brie. Besides, dogs need lunch too. How's he supposed to dance if he's starving?"

Cupid hadn't starved a day in his life. Erin chased after him. And if he kept eating like this, he'd be too fat to dance. She picked him up and tucked him under her arm.

"Yo, people!" It was Zach, Suze, and Rachel. Miss Pickering too. Cupid squirmed out of Erin's arms and ran up to her. Erin joined Nicola and Raelene.

She didn't want to talk to Rachel. Not now, not later, and especially not when she was with Suze.

The room quickly filled up with bodies. About a billion of them, Erin thought glumly. It was the rainy weather. People didn't want to go outside, so they'd come to watch the training session instead.

Just what she needed—an audience.

At least the crowd didn't bother Cupid. He tore around the room like a five-year-old in a candy store. Erin bent down and snapped her fingers. Ignoring her, he launched himself onto a desk and stuck his head in the open end. Only his back end was visible. It stuck into the air like a big, hairy balloon. The kids started to laugh. Even Erin giggled.

"Cupid!" she called. "Come here, boy."

But he burrowed farther into the desk, his behind wiggling as he went. Everyone howled.

"Cupid! Get out of there!" Miss Pickering marched over and pulled him out. But not before he managed to swallow what looked like a piece of day-old crust. "You have to stop eating so much!" Miss Pickering scolded.

Cupid licked his chops.

"No feeding Cupid anymore," Miss Pickering said. "As of this minute, he's on a diet. He needs to lose weight."

Zach materialized beside Erin. "Hey, how's it going?"

Amazing now that you're here. "Good," she said, crossing her arms to cover the hole in her sweater.

"Should we get Miss Pickering to dance with Cupid or do you want to try first?"

Erin pretended to consider. Instead her only thought was that Zach Cameron was staring at her with his amazing goldish brown eyes and asking *her* what she wanted to do. And he was standing so close she could smell his cologne again too. It was going to her head and making her think stupid things, like how his arm had felt around her the other day, how they had fit together. She stepped back, took a breath. "I...ah...I'll dance with Cupid," she said. "I'll try the same music because he knows it and he already has some moves. But let's slow it down, see if that helps his rhythm." It was like she was in a dream, watching herself talk. The words came out clear, confident. So not her.

"Oh, and Zach?" When he stopped and turned back to look at her, Erin felt a jolt of power. *Zach Cameron was waiting for her to speak.* "Deryk should tape the session so we can watch later and see where Cupid is having problems."

He smiled. "Good idea."

Good idea. He said it was a good idea!

When the familiar up-tempo South American beat filled the room a few minutes later, Erin's heart thumped along with the music. So many people staring at her. Including Deryk Latham with the school camcorder.

Never mind, she told herself. *Focus on the moves. On Cupid.* She concentrated on remembering Miss Pickering's steps. Tap left. Rock back. Swing forward.

So far, so good. She glanced down at Cupid. The dog was listening, watching, waiting for his cue.

When the time was right, Erin gave it to him. She snapped her fingers. Deryk Latham moved close with the camcorder.

That's when Cupid howled.

He ran under a desk, stuck his brown and white behind in the air, put his head between his paws, and howled at the camcorder.

Erin stopped. What was he doing?

"Don't worry, m'dear." Miss Pickering retrieved Cupid and placed him at Erin's feet. "He gets ornery sometimes."

They tried it again. Only this time when Erin snapped her fingers to give him his cue and Deryk moved in with the camcorder, Cupid didn't run under the chair and howl. He ran to Miss Pickering, cowered between her legs, and yelped and barked and howled like someone was torturing him.

They tried it four more times, and each time was the same. Cupid hated the camcorder.

"He's scared of the camcorder," Deryk said when they finally gave up. "We need to get him used to it, otherwise we won't have anything to send in."

This never would have happened if they'd chosen Blue, Erin thought miserably.

"It's only Monday," Zach said, joining them. Erin saw Suze watching from across the room. "We have all week."

That was the problem. They *only* had a week. It took months to properly train a dog. Zach had trained Lucille. He knew that.

"The music's not working either," Erin said. She didn't even want to think about the problem with the camcorder. "It's too fast. We need to pick out something else."

Deryk wandered away. Suze started toward them. Rachel and Madison trailed behind.

"Why don't we get together tonight?" Zach suggested. "We'll listen to some music then."

Why didn't they get together tonight? Because it was a school night, that's why, and her parents practically tied her down on school nights.

"We could go to Sweet Rosie's after dinner," Zach added. "I'll bring some CDs and my player."

Sweet Rosie's was where all the cool kids hung out. Everybody would see her with Zach!

"We could pick out some music," he continued. "And share a Chocolate Brownie Blast."

Share? As in eat from the *same dish*?

"What's this about a Chocolate Brownie Blast?" Suze asked, joining them.

"Erin and I are going to Sweet Rosie's tonight."

Zach made it sound like *a date*. Suze stared at her. Color flooded Erin's cheeks. But then Zach said, "We need to talk about Cupid's training session and pick out some new music."

"Huh," Suze said coolly. Her head whipped back

and forth between Erin and Zach. "I see." Her gaze dropped to the hole in Erin's sweater; her eyebrows rose. Erin crossed her arms again.

"The rain's supposed to stop," Zach said. "I could come by about seven. We could walk."

Erin caught the look of outright hostility on Suze's face. She had a moment of unease, but then she recalled those horrible things Suze had said in the bathroom. Her unease dissolved. This, she decided, was payback.

"Okay?" Zach prompted.

Her parents had to say yes. They just *had* to. "That would be great." Erin smiled at Zach. "I'll be ready."

"Good luck trying to find something from this century to wear," Suze murmured softly after Zach left. Madison giggled. Rachel started to speak, but Erin walked away. Rachel was a traitor. Whatever she had to say didn't interest Erin. Besides, she had a date with Zach Cameron to prepare for.

Providing her parents said yes.

When the doorbell rang later that night, Erin was in the middle of trying on her fifth shirt.

"Come in, Zach," she heard her father say.

Erin's eyes shot to her clock. He was *early*? Guys were supposed to be *late*.

What was she going to wear?

Desperate to save Zach from her father's questions, she threw her yellow shirt down and grabbed her first choice: a pale turquoise baby doll top trimmed with creamy lace. She pulled it on over her jeans, touched her lips with Pink Perfection lipstick, and spritzed her wrists with the *Diva* perfume Rachel had given her for Christmas. Then she grabbed a few of the CDs she'd selected and, with her heart thrumming, headed for the living room.

Zach gave her a nervous grin and bounced gently from one foot to another. "Hi."

"Hi." Zach Cameron was *really* at her house. Really picking *her up.* And he looked different, with his white denim shirt and a brown leather jacket instead of his usual gray soccer jersey. There was a pressure in Erin's chest that made it hard to breathe. *Don't blow this.* She repeated the words like a mantra. *Stay cool.*

"I brought some CDs."

Zach flashed open his jacket. "Me too." Erin glimpsed several CDs poking out of his pocket.

She grabbed her coat from the back of the couch, picked up her portable CD player, and said, "Let's go then."

"Be home—" her mom began.

"By nine thirty, I know."

"Not a minute later," her dad said firmly.

Erin hustled Zach out the door. "It won't be a problem," Zach said over his shoulder. "I have to be home by ten."

"You do?" She led him down the stairs to the sidewalk.

"Nah." A devilish grin crossed his face. "I can go home pretty much whenever I want, but it's the kind of stuff parents like to hear."

This was Zach Cameron talking?

"Don't worry, though. I'll have you home in time."

Suddenly conscious of the fact that she didn't know Zach Cameron all that well, Erin found herself at a loss for words.

They headed west on Ninth Street toward Lonsdale. Erin heard the muted sounds of traffic in the distance; she saw the golden glow from the streetlights casting shadows everywhere.

"I'm really worried about Cupid." She tried not to bump Zach's arm as they walked down the street.

He smiled; his teeth gleamed in the moonlight. "I can tell."

"He only wants to listen to Miss Pickering."

"Because he's bonded with her. Maybe you should

spend some extra time with him. Away from the training sessions. Take him for walks or something."

How was she supposed to fit that in with everything else she had to do?

"He'd get to know you better."

Zach was right. Maybe she could walk Cupid before school a few days a week. "It'll still be a challenge training him in a week. Especially to another piece of music."

"My mom says a dance routine is just a series of tricks strung together with music."

It sounded like something Grandma Morris would say. "Your mom's right," Erin said. "But Cupid needs to concentrate, and today was a bust."

"Too many people showed up," Zach said.

"We can't close the sessions completely. Cupid has to get used to people around when he does his routine." *With you training him, Cupid just might make the finals.* Okay, so maybe Rachel was trying to trick her, but there was a chance Cupid *could* make the finals. And if he did, he'd be performing in front of a crowd.

"We also need to get him used to the camcorder," Zach said. "And I don't know how to do that."

"Me either," Erin admitted. "Somehow we have to show him it's nothing to be afraid of."

Lost in their own thoughts, they fell silent. A few minutes later Erin caught sight of their shadows stretching up the sidewalk. It startled her. There was Zach, tall and slim, with his huge shoulders and long legs. And there she was, just a teeny bit shorter, walking beside him. A guy she liked was actually taller than her.

And she was *going on a date* with him. The thought almost made her trip.

"You okay?"

"Fine."

She had to get over herself. She couldn't walk to Sweet Rosie's in total silence. So she started talking, but not about Cupid. Talking about Cupid made her more nervous. Instead, she asked him questions about soccer, about school, about dogs. And by the time they reached Sweet Rosie's, Erin had almost relaxed, although when she saw the two of them reflected in the door, she tensed up again.

The guy was so hot he practically made her drool.

"Wanna share that Chocolate Brownie Blast?" Zach held the door open.

"Sure." Erin led the way inside.

Sweet Rosie's was crowded with kids. They clustered at the order counter, at the wrought-iron tables by the window, and in some of the booths at the back.

"There you are!" a voice cried out.

Erin's stomach dropped to her feet. She knew who *that* was.

She and Zach turned around at the same time. Suze waved from one of the back booths. She was surrounded by Madison, Steve, Nathan, and Rachel, who gave Erin a tiny shrug of her shoulders.

What were *they* doing here?

Chapter Nine

"WE THOUGHT WE'D COME and help pick out some music," Suze said after she and Zach had placed their order and picked up their Brownie Blast.

They were crammed together in the last red leather booth at Sweet Rosie's. The black and silver table between them was littered with shakes and fries and a half-eaten pizza. Erin made room for the CD player in the middle of the table.

"I phoned to warn you," Rachel whispered. Erin was pushed up beside her. "But you'd already left."

Erin didn't answer. She wouldn't even glance sideways.

"We need to talk," Rachel added softly.

No, they didn't. Rachel jabbed her in the waist; Erin jumped. "Stop it!" she hissed before turning her back and gesturing to the tower of brownie and ice cream on the table in front of her. "Shall we dig in?"

Zach sat across from her, squished in beside Suze. "For sure." He handed her a spoon.

"Me too!" Suze grabbed another spoon. "I just love sharing." She grinned innocently at Erin. "Don't you?"

Though she wanted to flip whipped cream in her face, Erin pretended not to care. She ate, she laughed at everybody's jokes, and she made a big effort not to look at Rachel. Finally, when all that was left of the Brownie Blast was a puddle of caramel sauce, she reminded them that they needed to find a new piece of music for Cupid.

"Can't we forget about that?" Suze asked.

"Stay with the Salsa," Nathan suggested. "It works fine."

But Erin wouldn't be deterred. Neither, she noticed with satisfaction, would Zach. Amidst the laughter and the cracks about "corpulent Cupid," she and Zach began listening to their selections. They knew what they were looking for—something similar to the Salsa but a little slower.

Unfortunately nothing jumped out at them.

It was hard to tell what they were even listening to, Erin thought as another burst of laughter drowned out the music. If they cranked the CD player up, the manager at Sweet Rosie's might kick them out, so they'd deliberately kept the volume down. But it was hard to hear with everyone talking.

"What do you think?" Zach asked as they bent

forward to listen to a hip-hop number he thought had potential. When Erin shook her head, he popped the CD out and put it back in its case.

"Maybe we should stick with the Salsa," she said with a sigh. "Cupid is already doing a few moves to it. If I can teach him a few more, he'll have enough for the contest." He'd have enough moves, but he wouldn't look great doing them. The Salsa piece was simply too fast for Cupid's little legs.

Suze popped another CD into the player and turned up the volume. "What about this?" "Feed Me Luv", the new Tawp Dawg song began playing.

Erin listened to the upbeat lyrics.

> *Feed me luv, in any way you can.*
> *Feed me luv, I'll be at your command.*
> *I'll be your slaveman,*
> *Your caveman,*
> *Your Superman*
> *Through the rest of time.*
> *If you'll just feed me, feed me, feed me luv.*

Erin looked at Zach. The beat was about right. The lyrics were cute, too. And Cupid was always ready to be fed. Although he'd take real food over love any day of the week.

"It would be great if you could get Cupid to dance to that!" Madison said.

"No kidding." Steve's red hair bounced as he moved his head in time to the beat. "Tawp Dawg is performing for the winning school, remember. They might see the submissions. Maybe even have a say in who makes the short list." He grinned. "It never hurts to suck up."

The words of the chorus floated over the table.

I will walk on ice for you.

I will fly through fire, it's true.

I'll be all that I can be

As long as you're there right next to me.

So feed me, feed me, feed me luv.

"What do you think?" Zach asked.

"It has potential," Erin said. It didn't just have potential, it was perfect. As much as she hated to admit it, Suze Shillington had found the right piece of music.

Zach tapped his fingers on the table. "Could you get Cupid to dance to it, though?"

Erin could see the moves in her mind. A slide through her legs to mimic walking on ice, a jump over her arm to imply flying through fire. "It's worth a try," she said as the song stretched into another chorus.

"Then it's settled! And congratulations to me because I found Cupid his music," Suze bragged.

Which was, Erin decided as they gathered up their things, both good and bad. Bad that Suze had found it. Good that they had something to work with. Bad that she only had a week to teach Cupid the moves.

They walked most of the way home as a group. Twice Rachel tried to speak to her. Twice Erin rebuffed her. There wasn't anything left to say. Even as she and Zach said good-bye to the others at the end of Erin's street, she was careful not to look Rachel in the eye.

"I had fun tonight," Zach said.

She would have had a lot more fun if Suze Shillington hadn't shown up. "Me too." At least they'd found a piece of music for Cupid.

"That was a great suggestion Suze made."

"It was." And she'd probably never let them forget it, either.

"I'll talk to Ratman about limiting the number of people at the training session." They stopped in front of Erin's house.

"Okay." He was standing so close she could smell the chocolate on his breath, she could see a tiny piece of maraschino cherry stuck between his two front teeth.

His eyes swept her face, lingered on her lips, and

for a heart-stopping second, she thought he might kiss her. Her knees trembled at the idea.

"Oh, by the way, I've been meaning to ask you." He hesitated and looked almost embarrassed.

Zach Cameron embarrassed? What was *this* about?

"My mom wanted me to get Lola's number from you. She's pretty excited that someone else wants to breed setters."

Erin's heart lurched. "Lola?"

"Yeah, Lola. Your friend on the island."

Her heart sped up to triple time. *Lola.* Oh crap. Now what?

"Oh right. Lola. I…um…think she's away." She felt the telltale prickle starting at the back of her neck. The porch light was on; he was going to see her blush.

"Away?"

"In…in Mexico."

"Is she still thinking of breeding setters?"

"Um. I don't know. I think so. Maybe." The prickle on her neck spread. Her cheeks grew warm. "But Chihuahuas too, I think. Which is why they're down there. Looking at them."

"Those things are ugly. I thought she loved setters. Didn't she have one when she was a baby?"

"She does. I mean, she did. But she said something about purse size. I mean, Lola's mom did. Because she talks. Not like Lola who is...who has that...you know...that mute thing going on. But her mom was thinking maybe a purse-size dog. And setters, well, they don't fit in purses. Unless they are puppies. And the purse is huge. Like backpack size. You know."

A tiny frown wrinkled Zach's forehead. "Are you okay?"

Her face was on fire. "I...um...yeah, I'm fine." She bolted up the stairs to the front door. Zach followed. "It's just...well, I don't really agree with Lola's thing—I mean her mom's thing...with Chihuahuas, so it's kinda hard for me to talk about it, plus it's 9:31 and I need to get inside or my parents will kill me." Right now, she wished they *would* kill her.

"I should go too. Just get me Lola's number, okay?"

"I will, but not tonight." Zach looked confused. He was going to ask her why not. When he opened his mouth, Erin rushed to say something, *anything* before he could.

"It's late and I...uh...have to study and my... address book is kinda missing and it'll take me a while to find it...and stuff."

"In the next couple of days though, okay? My mom's planning a trip to the island soon and she wants to meet Lola and her family. Since they want to breed setters, she might offer them a deal on two puppies. If she likes what she sees."

What if she didn't like what she saw? Because there was nothing to *see?* Erin pawed through her purse. *Where* was her key?

"And they'll be able to communicate too 'cause Mom can sign, which is great."

It was great all right. Her whole life was great. *A great big mess*. Had she forgotten her key? Was she going to have to ring the bell and show Zach what a total loser she was?

"Mom was crazy happy when she found out about Lola. Setters aren't that common a breed these days. Mom figures that with Lola she might be able to start a setter comeback."

A setter comeback. How about an *invisible* setter comeback? To match her *invisible* friend. Her fingers fastened on a piece of metal. It was her key. Hidden under a wad of tissues.

Zach leaned close; his breath tickled her cheek. "You'll just have to convince Lola that Chihuahuas suck and setters rule."

No problem, Erin thought as Zach turned,

waved, and headed down the stairs. She could convince Lola of anything. Because friends like Lola never talked back.

———————————— • ◯ ————

Erin had way too much on her mind to sleep. It was well after midnight when she fell into a restless slumber. Then she had a nightmare about a headless woman named Lola, who was teaching a red setter with a bulldog head how to dance to "Feed Me Luv". She woke up in a cold sweat.

Her life was one great big *huge* disaster. Thanks to Rachel. Her first priority had to be disaster control.

That meant avoiding Zach Cameron at any cost.

She couldn't talk about Lola. And she couldn't keep lying. If she didn't see him, there was no chance of either happening.

Getting to school early was one way to avoid him. Plus, it would give her a chance to bond with Cupid.

———————————— • ◯ ————

"Would you mind if I walked Cupid every day before school?" Erin asked Miss Pickering the next morning. The school secretary was making the first pot of coffee. Cupid jumped up and sniffed Erin's hand. He probably smelled the bacon she had for breakfast. "I won't go far. Just to the rocks."

"Good idea. More exercise might help him lose

weight." After flipping the switch on the coffee machine, Miss Pickering pulled Cupid's red leash from the bottom desk drawer.

Cupid's tiny ears flattened; he bolted across the floor and hid under the copy machine. "He's not a fan of walks," she said, hauling the dog out by the collar and snapping his leash in place.

No kidding, Erin thought, dragging Cupid through the field to the rocks. The grass was wet and muddy from the recent rain. Cupid stepped through it like it was pig slop. When it got really muddy, she took pity on him and carried him the rest of the way.

"Don't tell anyone. You're supposed to be getting exercise."

Cupid was happier on hard, dry ground. His ears perked up, his tail wagged; he snuffled and snarfled at tree trunks and leaves. Erin wanted him to relax and enjoy himself, so she let him set the pace. While he walked, she listened to "Feed Me Luv" over and over on her portable CD player. By the time the bell rang and students started drifting across the field to the school, Erin had a good idea of how their dance routine should go.

That was one stress off her mind at least. All she had to do now was teach Cupid the routine. And avoid Zach.

With that in mind, Erin waited until the last possible minute to return Cupid to the office.

"There you are," Miss Pickering said when Erin appeared. "I was beginning to worry."

"He was enjoying the fresh air," Erin said as she deposited Cupid in his bed under Miss Pickering's desk.

The sound of a familiar voice floated out from Mr. Ratzka's office. "No, sir. I didn't see a thing."

It was Zach Cameron.

Miss Pickering misunderstood the horrified look on Erin's face. "It's awful, isn't it?" When Erin didn't answer, she continued. "Another theft." She clucked her teeth together. "This time it's a pair of glasses from Mr. Ponchet's room."

"I didn't see a thing," Zach continued. "I was the last one to leave the room. Of course I'll watch. For sure."

Shock kept Erin rooted to the spot. Zach had left the room before her...hadn't he?

"Mr. Ratzka wants to keep this latest theft quiet," Miss Pickering murmured. "We think someone is stealing for the attention. The fewer people who know about the glasses, the better." When Erin nodded, she added, "You will let us know if you see anything suspicious, won't you, dear?"

"Of course." Erin strained to hear the rest of the conversation in Mr. Ratzka's office, but Miss Pickering's voice distracted her.

"I feel somewhat responsible," the secretary continued, "because Mrs. Abernathy's bracelet and now Mr. Ponchet's glasses went missing when Cupid was dancing. But poor Zach." She looked at Mr. Ratzka's door. "He must feel wretched. As head of the Special Events Committee, he's responsible for everything that happens during the session. And he's supposed to be the last person out of the room."

Erin pondered that bit of information walking to her locker. She'd left right after Suze's nasty comment about her clothes. And Zach had left before her. She was sure he had. He must have returned to the multi-purpose room. If he said he was the last one to leave the room, then it had to be true. Because guys like Zach Cameron didn't lie.

Unlike a certain girl who had an imaginary friend named Lola.

Chapter Ten

RACHEL WAS AWAY; ERIN WAS RELIEVED. That meant fewer chances to run into her and Suze together. She had Cupid to worry about. Even though she'd worked out the dance routine in her mind, it was going to be a challenge teaching it to him when he was so afraid of the camcorder. During social studies, she tried to convince Mona to help.

"I don't know anything about dogs," Mona whispered when the teacher's back was turned. "Plus I'm training for a skateathon. Besides, why waste your time with Cupid?"

The teacher turned around and Erin couldn't answer. There were lots of reasons. One, she'd been roped into it and she couldn't back out. Two, people were paying more attention to her. As she'd walked to social studies, three kids from Zach's crowd had said hi. But there was another reason too.

"Cupid might make the finals," she whispered to

Mona the next time the teacher looked away. "You never know."

Mona just shook her head. "I still can't help. Sorry."

Trying to convince Mona had been a long shot, Erin knew that. Still, she was disappointed.

She was even more disappointed when she walked into the multi-purpose room at lunch and found Suze and Deryk alone and yelling at each other. Mona's calmness would have diffused the situation.

"Don't be such a loser, Latham. That's a stupid idea!"

"You're the loser, Shillington. It's not a stupid idea."

"You heard Miss Pickering." Suze's hands were on her hips; she glared. "We're not supposed to feed Cupid anything."

"This is a reward." Deryk shook the small red box he held in his hand. "It'll help him get used to the camcorder."

Suze snorted. "That's dumb. You're a dumb-ass, Latham."

No one deserved to be talked to that way. Erin marched over, snatched the box from Deryk's hand, and waved it under Suze's chin.

"Excuse me!" she said. Suze stepped back in surprise. "It's not dumb. It's called positive reinforcement and dog trainers use it all the time."

"Yeah," Deryk muttered.

She glanced at the box in her hand. Deryk had bought *diet* dog biscuits. Her opinion of him edged up a notch. She looked up, caught Deryk's eye, and smiled. "In fact, I should have thought of it myself."

"You should have thought of *what* yourself?"

It was Zach! Color flooded Erin's cheeks. She knew she'd see him at lunch; she'd tried to prepare herself. She'd even practiced what she'd say if he asked her about Lola: *She's ditched Ireland for Mexico. And setters for Chihuahuas. Sorry.*

But saying *anything* was practically impossible when he stood in front of her in those tight jeans and cream sweatshirt looking like some kind of God.

"Deryk wants to feed Cupid dog biscuits so he'll pay attention," Suze said before Erin could untangle her tongue. She sauntered to Zach's side, put her hand on his arm, and leaned in close. They looked good together. Too good, Erin thought. "Which is a totally stupid idea," Suze continued, "because the dog's overweight and Miss Pickering said we aren't supposed to feed him."

"Suze is right." Zach gave Deryk a look that

bordered on confrontational. "Scrap the biscuits, Latham."

Deryk glowered. If Suze had been a cat she would have purred with pleasure. Instead, she only smirked.

The dog biscuits were a brilliant idea. As a dog owner Zach should know that. The thought of disagreeing made Erin squirm. But she had to say *something*.

"Uh, Zach, I think Deryk's idea is a good one." Three pairs of eyes swiveled in her direction. "When you train a dog, you play to his strengths. Cupid loves food. If we put a biscuit by the camcorder, he'll focus on it. We don't have to give him lots. I'll talk to Miss Pickering. Besides." She handed Zach the box. "Deryk bought *diet* biscuits."

Zach didn't even look down. Instead he said, "Let's forget the camcorder for today and give Cupid a chance to get used to the new music."

"Let's not," Deryk said. His hands were curled into fists at his side. "Cupid needs to get used to the camcorder."

Zach glared at him.

What was with those two? Erin wondered. They'd accomplish nothing if they spent the next five days fighting. She tried to smooth things over.

"You both have a point. Cupid needs to get used to the music *and* the camcorder. But we don't have much time."

That led to a discussion about schedules and conflicts: Erin had her shifts at the SPCA. Deryk had archery; Zach had soccer. They agreed to record the video Friday afternoon. That way, they could courier it downtown in time for Monday morning.

"I'll write the letter to go with our submission," Suze suggested. When Nicola offered to help her, the two girls headed for the computer station in the corner.

"I'll cue up the song," Zach said after Miss Pickering dropped Cupid off.

Only half a dozen people had shown up for today's session. Erin hoped the smaller group would make things easier. Cupid already moved forward and back to music, but she needed to see if he would do it to "Feed Me Luv". If there was time, she wanted to try the slide and jump move.

Unfortunately, all Cupid wanted to try were the dog biscuits.

Eventually, Erin put one in her pocket, which kept Cupid glued to her side. The tune was perfect; Erin's dance routine seemed to be working. Best of all, when she held the biscuit in her fist and guided it in front of Cupid's nose, the dog moved in time to "feed me, feed me, feed me luv".

"I can't believe it," Zach said when Erin called for a break. "He's doing way better than I expected."

"It's the song," Suze called from across the room. "I told you he'd love it."

Steve rolled his eyes. "It's not the song at all. Cupid wants the biscuits, that's all." Zach laughed.

After the break, they brought out the camcorder and put a biscuit on top. Cupid was wary but eventually he did part of the routine. Near the end of lunch hour, he even did his first slide and dead dog pose!

But he only did it once. No matter how hard Erin tried, he wouldn't do the slide a second time.

"He's doing great for the first day," Zach said as they packed everything up.

It was true. Cupid liked the song, and the beat was perfect for his stance. "He has to learn some other moves," Erin said. "I want to get him to do a jump and a slide at the end."

Zach shrugged. "He doesn't need to learn the *whole* routine. As long as he does a few of the tricks. We can fake up the rest."

Fake up the rest? Alarm prickled Erin's neck.

"Fake what?" Suze asked, joining them.

"I said as long as Cupid does a few of the moves, we can fake up the rest."

You have to stand up for yourself. Her mom's words floated through her mind. *And learn to say no once in a while.* "I don't want to fake anything," Erin said.

Suze looked amused. "You can always teach Cupid the rest of the routine once we send the video. That way if he makes the finals, he'll be ready."

"Not if. When." Zach grinned.

"Oh, I forgot." This time, Suze's smile held no warmth. "He's being trained by the official dog whisperer of Carson Heights, right?"

"That's right." Erin refused to drop her gaze. Suze, finally, looked away first.

"Hey, did you find Lola's number?" Zach asked. "Mom's been bugging me about it."

Erin felt the all-too-familiar flush start. Why did he have to ask in front of Suze? "Actually, I, uh, didn't look because she emailed me." Suze was staring; there was no *way* she'd crack that joke about Ireland and Mexico now. "She's decided to stick with Chihuahuas. I called to try and talk her out of it, but her brother said she's still down there and I haven't had time to call back."

"Too busy shopping for the perfect outfit for the routine, I'll bet." When Erin was silent, Suze continued. "Let me know if I can help." She linked her arm through Zach's and gave Erin's clothes a dismissive once-over. "I'm good with impossible cases." Giggling, she led Zach away.

Erin's heart fell. The insult was one thing, but Lola again? She hated lying to Zach.

She also hated Zach's suggestion that she fake it. She hadn't thought he was that kind of guy. But then, she hadn't thought Zach Cameron was the kind of guy to shirk his responsibilities either. And he obviously was. Because as Erin followed Deryk Latham out the door, she realized Zach hadn't stuck around like he was supposed to. He wasn't the last person to leave Mr. Ponchet's room.

And he'd given his word to Mr. Ratzka that he would be.

Erin sprawled out on top of her quilt with Blue at her feet. She wasn't supposed to have him on the bed, but who cared?

What was she going to tell Zach if he kept bugging her about Lola? How could she admit she was fake? And what if he kept insisting she fake up the video with Cupid? Sighing, she reached over and ran her fingers over Blue's soft, black coat. She'd gotten tricked into faking an imaginary friend, but she wouldn't fake the video. She knew that for sure.

"Erin?" Her dad banged on her door.

"What?"

He stuck his head inside her room, held out the phone. "You can't keep ignoring Rachel. This is the sixth time she's called in thirty minutes."

Rachel had called yesterday too. Over and over again.

"You need to deal with this," her dad said again.

Wordlessly, Erin held out her hand. She flopped back onto her pillow, tucked her feet under Blue's back, and held the receiver to her ear. When her dad left the room, she said one word: "Speak."

"Don't hang up," Rachel said. In a rush she explained that Erin hadn't heard the whole conversation between her and Suze in the bathroom, that she *did* think Erin was the best person to train Cupid and no, she *wasn't* out to humiliate her and she *did* think Erin had friends and she'd been telling Suze that when the toilet flushed, which is why Erin hadn't heard it.

The only problem was that Rachel sounded like she was talking under water. She had Keegan's cold.

"Erin?" Rachel paused. "Are you there?"

"I'm here."

Another pause. "I'm reabby, reabby sorry."

She was really, really sorry. Erin got it.

"It wasn't what you think," Rachel said.

"Right."

"I don't know what else to say. Except I'b reabby sorry."

Erin was really sorry too. About her entire life. "Zach keeps asking about Lola," she finally said.

"Oh."

"I've tried to get him to stop." She told Rachel about her Chihuahua brainwave. "But if he keeps asking, I might have to tell." The thought made her light-headed. Although what was worse? Maintaining the lie or admitting she'd lied in the first place? She slid her feet farther under Blue. He was a heavy, comforting weight against her ankles.

"You can't tell."

"Why not?"

"He'll think you're a loober, that's why."

It didn't matter how you said it. She *was* a loser. And a loober. Big-time on both counts. "I can't lie about this, Rache. It's not right."

"Look, after he asks you out and sees how honest you are *norbally*, then you tell hib and laugh and he'll think it's cute. But not now!"

"How can I stall him off?"

"You'll figure sombthig out."

"No, Rache. *You'll* figure something out because you got me into this mess in the first place and I have enough other messes to deal with right now." Like Cupid, who had only done that spin once. And algebra, which was the curse of the civilized world.

There was silence on the other end of the phone. "Okay," Rachel finally said. "You tell him that there was a massib hurricane in Mexico and Lola stayed behind to help wib the orphans because her mom's coordinating the relief effort and—"

"Raaachel!"

"Okay, okay." More silence. "Tell him that Lola not only changed her mind, but her mother is moobing the whole family to Mexico and they're not coming back. That should shut him up."

It was another lie, but at least it didn't involve hurricanes and orphans and relief efforts. And it would get Lola out of the picture forever. One more lie on top of a whole bunch. "I think I'm gonna tell him nothing and just try to avoid him."

"That'll neber work."

That'll never work. "Why not?"

"Erin, wake up and smell your dating life."

"It doesn't smell."

"That's my point. It doesn't smell because it doesn't *exist*. Avoiding Zach accomplishes nothing.

Why waste your time making that vibeo if you aren't going to get anything out of it?"

"You said the other day that Cupid might make the short list. Or were you just trying to make me feel better?"

"No," Rachel insisted. "I meant it!"

Did she? Erin wasn't sure about Rachel anymore.

"Don't avoid Zach," Rachel said. "Just tell him one more lie and be done with it."

Tell him one more lie and be done with it. Did she even know Rachel anymore? "I don't get it, Rachel. You used to be so honest."

"I still am. Mostly. Except when it comes to guys. Then, all's fair in lub and war. Besides, this isn't a big deal. It's not hurting anyone."

Not true. It hurt her. Lying to Zach was a great big pain in the neck. It made her queasy. And a little bit ashamed. Knowing she wouldn't get anywhere arguing, Erin changed the subject. She gave Rachel the details about the English essay that was due next Tuesday, and she filled her in on the latest with Cupid.

Finally, as the conversation wound to a close, Rachel apologized again and asked Erin if everything was okay. "Yes," Erin said before hanging up. And things *were* okay. Not great, just okay.

Nothing was great anymore. Nothing at all.

Chapter Eleven

ERIN SLEPT ON HER PROBLEM. What to tell Zach? How to tell Zach? Should she even tell him at all? By morning, she decided to say nothing.

If he asked again, she would tell him that Lola had given up on setters *for sure* and Erin was too busy to call and try to change her mind.

Which was true. She was too busy training Cupid. It was Wednesday. They were shooting the video Friday. And they were nowhere near ready. She simply told Zach, Deryk, and Suze that she needed training time alone with Cupid. She proposed a dry run at noon Friday, followed by the actual taping after school that day.

The pressure was on. She had only two days to pull Cupid's routine together.

Unfortunately, Wednesday was a complete disaster. Mr. Ratzka was on a rant because a letter opener was missing from the library. Ms. Carter did a full review in algebra, but instead of helping Erin, it confused her more. But worst of all, Cupid refused to cooperate. He wouldn't go sideways, he wouldn't spin. He wouldn't even eat the diet dog biscuits.

Erin wanted to scream. Rachel had gotten her into this mess. Why couldn't she come and help her deal with it?

But Rachel was sick. Besides, she didn't know anything about dance routines or dogs.

After school, Erin talked to Mona again. To her relief, Mona agreed to help. Thursday, on the way to school, Erin bought a huge box of high fat bacon-flavored biscuits with extra large cheddar chunks. Cupid would probably love them.

He did.

As long as she held one of the high-fat biscuits, Cupid paid attention. He went forward and back, he pranced sideways, he did the spin like he'd been doing it forever. "I swear, he's showing off for you." Erin giggled as Cupid blinked his big brown eyes at Mona. His tongue lolled out; he looked like he was grinning.

"Whatever it takes." Mona grinned back. "Try throwing the biscuit in the air again." She cued up the song.

That was the clincher. If she could get him to do

the jump *and* the slide in order, they'd be home free. As soon as Tawp Dawg broke into the line "I will fly through fire, it's true," Erin tossed a piece of biscuit and flipped her arm.

Without missing a beat, Cupid jumped into the air and retrieved it. Erin tossed another bit on the floor; he ended on a slide! She couldn't believe it. In fact, she was so thrilled with Cupid's progress, she asked Deryk Latham to tape them after school.

"You sure about this?" Deryk eyed Cupid skeptically.

Erin quickly shut the door to the multi-purpose room. She didn't want Zach or Suze showing up. "Trust me." She dug the CD out of her backpack. "He's okay with the camcorder as long as you don't get too close. I need to watch the tape later and see where we can improve."

Although she wasn't sure when she'd find the time. She had a shift at the SPCA tonight and she still had to study for tomorrow's algebra test.

"I rubbed the camcorder with some biscuit crumbs." Erin was careful to be gentle, not to leave scratches. "See?" she said a minute later when Cupid waddled over and sniffed the camcorder.

Deryk grinned. "And you ditched the diet cookies and bought better ones." When Cupid licked the camcorder, Deryk's grin deepened. He was kind of cute when he smiled, Erin thought.

They worked with Cupid for more than an hour. Half the time he did the jump and half the time he didn't. But he only did the slide once. And even then, he didn't do a very good job of it.

"I'll dump the slide," Erin told Deryk as they walked Cupid back to the office. "I'll get him to go from the final jump to a spin and then into the dead dog pose." She played the routine out in her head. The slide would have been better, but Cupid couldn't handle the transition. The spin would have to do.

Erin watched Cupid on tape while she ate dinner. *Not bad*, she thought, noting what looked fine and what didn't. By the time she arrived at the SPCA, she felt pretty good. The two-minute video wouldn't be a problem.

But algebra was another thing altogether.

"How's it coming?" Richard asked when he walked into the reception area later that night and saw Erin sitting behind the desk studying.

"It's coming." She closed her book with a sigh. "I have the test tomorrow, but don't worry, every-thing's done. The cages are clean, the animals have been watered, the paperwork's caught up."

"We don't mind you studying when it's quiet."

Richard leaned over to scratch Peaches's head. The cocker spaniel was curled up in Erin's lap. "By the way, how are things going with Cupid?"

She knew Richard didn't approve of the contest. But that was one of the things she liked about him—he didn't force his beliefs on others. "Better than I expected," she said. "Although I can't get him to do the slide."

"Don't push him," Richard said. "Go easy."

"I'll be careful." Erin put her algebra notes in her knapsack and packed up her things.

Friday, she woke up tired and cranky. She was worried about the test, worried about making Cupid's video, and *really* worried about avoiding Zach.

Luckily, she didn't run in to him during the morning. And Rachel was still away so she didn't see her either. Soon it was time to meet Deryk for the practice run.

"Cupid's already there," Miss Pickering said when Erin went to the office to pick him up. A tiny frown creased her forehead. "At least I think so. I sent him in that direction."

Cupid wandered the halls freely, especially when Miss Pickering was busy. The secretary told anyone who would listen that Cupid not only knew his way around the school but always followed her orders. He would go, she said, wherever she sent him. He was that smart. But everyone knew Cupid headed for one of two places—the cafeteria or the home-ec room, whichever smelled better.

So when Erin walked into the multi-purpose room and didn't see Cupid, she wasn't surprised. It was lunchtime. He was probably in the cafeteria. Then she heard a muffled rattle coming from behind Mr. Ponchet's desk. She went over, stood on her toes, and peered down.

Cupid's entire head was buried inside the box of dog biscuits.

"Cupid!" Horrified, Erin dashed around the desk, grabbed the box of dog treats, and pulled. Biscuits went flying. Cupid pounced on them, crunching and slurping.

"What's he doing?"

Talk about timing. It was Deryk.

"He's eating! What does it look like?" Erin snatched up as many of the stray biscuits as she could.

"He's eaten almost the whole box."

"Don't remind me. The dog has an eating disorder, remember?"

Cupid finished his feast and trotted over to sniff

the ground at Erin's feet. "They're all gone!" She glared and then put the box high up on a shelf. He wagged his stubby tail and licked the carpet.

Deryk chuckled.

"It's not funny!" She studied the dog nervously. "I hope he's going to be okay."

"He'll be fine," Deryk said. "Come on, let's do the dry run."

Cupid was raring to go. Clearly wanting another biscuit, he moved in time to the beat, although he was reluctant to do the jump and there was still no way he'd do the slide. "Let's try one last time," Erin said.

They cued the music and started the routine. Everything went well until it was time for the jump. Erin raised her hand to give him his cue. Cupid looked like he was ready to lift off and jump.

Instead, he lifted his head and threw up.

Stunned, Erin just stared. Deryk ran for paper towels.

She bent down and touched Cupid's nose. It was cool and wet. Thank goodness. "You ate too many biscuits, didn't you?" Gently she rubbed his forehead. Cupid belched. The smell made her reel back in disgust.

"What if I've poisoned him?" she asked when

Deryk came back.

"You haven't poisoned him." He began to clean up the mess. "It looks like he's thrown up that entire box. He'll probably be back to normal and eating again in an hour."

Deryk was wrong.

By 3:15, Cupid was sicker than ever.

"He's still not well," Miss Pickering said. The dog was on his blanket with his head between his paws. He moaned when Erin scratched behind his ear. "He's thrown up four times since two o'clock."

"It's my fault." Guilt flooded Erin. "He didn't like the diet biscuits so I bought bacon cheddar ones instead. He must have pulled the box from Mr. Ponchet's desk because it was practically empty when I got there!"

"Ah." Miss Pickering's frown faded. "Cupid is terribly sensitive to trans fats. He once ate three store-bought muffins and was sick for two days." She smiled reassuringly. "He'll be fine in a day or two, but he won't be making the video today."

Suze and Zach arrived in time to hear Miss Pickering's last few words. "Why not?" Zach asked.

"Cupid went crazy over the dog biscuits," Erin said when Miss Pickering answered the phone.

Suze shot Deryk a disgusted look. "I told you

140

they were a stupid idea."

"Yeah, Latham. Thanks to you we're gonna be scrambling to get that video in on time," Zach added.

Erin flushed and waited for Deryk to tell them that she'd exchanged the diet biscuits for ones loaded with way too many trans fats. But all he said as he shrugged on his black leather jacket and turned those pale blue eyes on Zach was, "Don't sweat the small stuff, Cameron. We'll do the video Sunday. I'll send it express courier. It'll still make it by Monday."

And then he was gone.

Before Erin had time to digest the fact that Deryk had saved her from embarrassment, Suze said, "I guess I'll cancel tonight's party."

Party? Erin wondered.

"There's no point if the video's not done."

"You know about Suze's party, don't you?" Zach asked.

"No."

Suze's eyes widened. "I told Rachel to tell you."

Yeah, right, Erin thought.

"It's at my place. After the video's done. Sunday now, I guess. You're welcome to come."

It didn't sound like she was welcome. It didn't

look like it either. Mostly because Suze was staring at Zach as she issued the invitation.

"You will come, won't you?" Zach asked. "I'll pick you up."

He would pick her up! Jealousy flickered in Suze's eyes. "I'll make my own way there." The last time Zach picked her up—or more specifically when he'd taken her home—he'd asked about Lola. She didn't want to give him that chance again.

"What time?"

"Seven o'clock, wasn't it?" Zach asked Suze.

"Something like that." She gave Zach a toothy grin before glancing at Erin. "I'll confirm the time and stuff on Sunday."

Knowing Suze, she might confirm by "uninviting" her again. But Erin didn't have time to dwell on that. She was too worried about Cupid.

What if she's poisoned him with those stupid biscuits? She hadn't poisoned Cupid, Miss Pickering reassured her when Erin called Friday night. What if she made a fool of herself at Suze's party? she asked when Rachel called a little later. She wouldn't, Rachel said. Rachel's cold was almost gone. She promised to be there for the taping. And of course for the party.

Saturday, Erin called Miss Pickering four times

from the SPCA. By midday, the secretary said Cupid was up and wandering around. By the time Erin got off shift and headed for the mall to buy a new top, Cupid was back to his old self, begging for food. "He'll be fine when you pick him up tomorrow," Miss Pickering said. "Don't worry."

Miss Pickering lived in a brown house about five blocks from Carson Heights. The heady scent of the purple lilacs floated through the air as Erin knocked on the front door Sunday morning.

"Oh, good. You're early!" Miss Pickering said, letting her in. "We'll have time to groom him. Cupid can be a little sensitive about the brush."

Sensitive was an understatement.

Even though he was in his own kitchen with his own yellow brush, the dog hated to be groomed. He jumped and thrashed and yipped and howled so much that he made Peaches look laid-back.

Eventually, they brushed his coat, treated his face wrinkles with a soothing gel, and cleaned his brown tear stains with a lanolin baby wipe.

"I wish I could do something with his jowls," Miss Pickering said when they finished. "Or maybe have his overbite corrected."

"Corrected?"

"Surgically, of course. Several of my friends have had their bulldogs done. But it's so expensive." She sighed. "It's simply not feasible on my salary."

Okay, so Cupid wasn't your classically good-looking dog, like Blue. But his jowls weren't so bad. Besides, Erin thought, stepping back and studying him, he was a teeny-weeny bit beautiful, in an ugly sort of way!

"Good luck, dear," Miss Pickering said as she waved good-bye. "The next stop is the final competition!"

Miss Pickering made it sound like Cupid would make it to the finals. Zach thought so too. Even Rachel said it was possible. But she had to be realistic, Erin reminded herself as she walked Cupid to Carson Heights. The chances of Cupid being short-listed were about as remote as winning the lottery.

The custodian was hovering inside the entrance-way when Erin arrived. "The rest of the group is already here." He let her in and locked the door behind her.

Erin flew down the deserted hall. The multi-purpose room wasn't crowded, but there were more people there than she would have liked. There was Suze, of course, with Zach, Madison, and Krista. Rachel was in the corner with Nathan, Steve, and Nicola. Erin waved as she unsnapped Cupid from his leash. He trotted over to Mr. Ponchet's desk and began sniffing the carpet.

Deryk materialized beside her. "He has a good memory." He fiddled with one of the switches on the camcorder.

"Yeah." Erin held her breath and waited for him to add something sarcastic. But he moved away instead. Why hadn't he told the others that she'd switched the dog biscuits? She didn't get it. The guy had been bugging her since grade five. Why the change now?

Erin didn't have time to dwell on Deryk. The cut-off for the courier was 4:00 p.m. That gave them only a couple of hours to get the video taped and edited.

They decided to tape Cupid doing the routine more than once. "That way we can pick the best one," Erin suggested. Everyone agreed. It took Cupid time to get warmed up, and he was easily distracted, so they ended up taking a few breaks too. Cupid disappeared after the second break, which left everyone panic-stricken. But Nathan found him wandering forlornly outside the closed cafeteria and brought him back.

They managed to get enough of Cupid on tape by 3:00. Erin wanted to stay and help with the editing, but she'd promised Miss Pickering that Cupid would be home before 3:30.

"Great job!" Zach said as she pulled Cupid's leash out of her jacket pocket.

Other voices chimed in.

"Yeah, nice one."

"Amazing what you managed to do with the corpulent one."

"You turned Cupid into a star, man."

Rachel grinned. Beside her, Suze managed a wan smile.

"So your party's at seven tonight?" Erin asked Suze.

"Yes, seven." Suze crossed her arms and Erin got the message: *you're only coming because you backed me into a corner.*

But Rachel looked unconcerned. "How about I pick you up at six-thirty?" she asked.

It was better than going alone. "Sure." Erin snapped Cupid's leash in place. "I'll see you at six-thirty."

Chapter Twelve

SUZE'S HOUSE WAS FANCIER than Rachel had described. Erin wasn't prepared for the cathedral ceilings, the butterscotch leather couches, and especially not the oversize hot tub on the deck. She hadn't brought her bathing suit.

"You should have told me," Erin complained as Rachel led her back to the kitchen. Music bounced off the walls; the smell of pizza and something vaguely sweet wafted through the air.

"I'm sorry," Rachel said. Bodies spilled out the patio doors onto the deck; people crowded into the hot tub. "I thought Suze mentioned it, otherwise I would have said something when I picked you up."

As Erin listened to the laughter and watched the splashing, she felt more and more out of place.

"Hey, you guys, you're just in time for pizza." Madison shoved a triangular wedge of cheesy pie into Erin's hands and gestured to the box on the counter. "Help yourself." She headed back outside.

"Where are Suze's folks?" Erin bit off a chunk of pepperoni.

Rachel shrugged, eyed the pizza. "They don't hang around much."

Her parents would kill her if they knew that. Erin watched Madison splash Zach when she jumped back in the tub. As it was, she'd had to do some fancy talking to go to a party on a Sunday night.

"You guys finally made it!" Suze wandered into the kitchen wearing a brilliant tankini and matching scarlet lipstick. "Rachel showed you around, right?" She didn't wait for an answer. Instead she asked, "Did she show you the refreshments?"

Nodding, Erin pointed to the soda bottles on the counter beside the pizza.

Suze giggled. "Not those, silly." With a flourish, she pulled open a set of doors. "These." Shock turned Erin cold. The cupboard was filled with beer, rum, vodka, and alcopops. Now Erin recognized that sweet smell. Beer. "There's cold beer in the fridge too. Lots to go around. Don't be shy, 'kay?" Suze poured some rum into a glass, added two ice cubes and cola, and wandered back to the patio.

Horrified, Erin turned to Rachel. "You didn't tell me there'd be drinking!"

Rachel wouldn't meet her eyes. "There isn't always. Only when Suze's brother buys it." She chewed her pizza, eventually met Erin's gaze. "Besides, you don't have to."

"Do you?"

Rachel was silent.

Erin took that as a yes. Disappointment slammed her like a fist to the gut. Rachel had changed. She wasn't the same person she'd been a year ago. Six months ago even. She hung around with the cool kids now. And did things Erin didn't like. "I need to go." Seconds later, Zach jumped out of the hot tub and headed for the kitchen.

"Hey, gorgeous, you made it!"

Gorgeous? Zach Cameron had called her gorgeous? Rachel gave her a sideways grin. *Zach Cameron had called her gorgeous.*

"Yeah, I made it." The words came out in one long whoosh.

"Zach! You're trailing water! Here." Suze threw him an oversize towel. "My parents will kill me if we get the floor wet."

"Sorry." Zach toweled off; Erin tried hard not to stare at his chest, his huge arms, that sprinkle of chest hair.

Tried and failed.

He tossed the towel onto a wicker chair. "Wanna beer?"

Zach drank too? He was big into athletics. What was up with *that*? Erin shook her head. Rachel said no. He grabbed one from the fridge, twisted off the cap, and turned to face them. "So what's the deal with Lola?" He leaned against the counter, gave Erin a smile the size of New York City.

Lola? Beside her, Rachel grew very still. "What do you mean?"

"My mom called your mom. Your mom said she didn't know any Lola." Zach took a long swig of beer.

Zach's mom called? Erin shot Rachel a panicked look. Rachel shrugged.

"She did?" Erin said weakly.

"Yeah." Zach's face was flushed; his brown eyes gleamed like two shiny new pennies. "I told Mom what you said about Lola deciding on Chihuahuas. She couldn't figure out how someone could pick a barking rodent over a setter. Especially since you said they'd had a setter when Lola was little and they wanted to start breeding them again. She wanted to call and talk to them before they made the mistake of their lives." He laughed. "So did you make her up or what?"

"Make who up?" Suze was heading for more alcohol.

Erin stared at Suze's glass. Had she finished that first one already?

"Loooola." Zach dragged out the first syllable with a laugh. Erin wondered how much he'd had to drink. "Erin's mute friend who wants to breed setters. Or was it Chihuahuas?"

Rachel started to speak but Suze interrupted her. "Aren't you a little old for imaginary friends, Erin?" Her glass full, she went to stand beside Zach.

Rachel snapped her mouth shut.

There was only one thing to do. Come clean and take the consequences. "Apparently not," Erin said coolly.

"Sad when you have so few friends that you have to make them up," Suze said with a nasty giggle.

"That's not funny," Rachel said sharply.

"Loooola," Suze drawled.

"Loooola," Zach repeated. They both dissolved into fits of laughter.

The pepperoni pizza flipped over in Erin's stomach. She wanted to disappear. Fast.

"Come on!" Rachel grabbed Erin's arm. "Let's get out of here."

Erin was sick. Sick, sick, sick. It didn't matter how much Rachel tried to reassure her on the walk home. She couldn't face Zach Cameron or Suze Shillington ever again.

"I think I have the flu," she told her mother when she woke up Monday morning. It was the same thing she'd said the night before. "A really bad case. It's probably going to last until school lets out in June."

Her mother had been surprisingly sympathetic when Erin had come home and explained the whole Lola mess. She'd known something was up when Zach's mother had called. After Erin explained everything, her mom repeated her favorite phrase: lying is easy, the truth is hard.

The truth was, now she had to go to school and face everybody.

And that *would* be hard.

Erin timed it so she arrived in homeroom as the announcements started. Rachel was watching the door, flicking her pale blonde hair back and forth the way she did when she was nervous or upset. As soon as she saw Erin, she grinned and gave her a tiny thumbs-up signal.

That was the only good thing to come out of the whole mess, Erin decided, sliding into her seat. Rachel had stood up for her. Sort of. She hadn't taken the rap for creating Lola, but she had stood up to Suze, and she had left the party with her. That counted for something.

The announcements were winding down when Mr. Ratzka said, "Would Erin Morris come to the office, please?"

Her heart did a rat-a-tat dance in her chest. What was going on?

"I wonder what's up?" Rachel pondered as they filed out of homeroom.

"No clue."

"Suze spoke to me this morning," she said.

"Huh." Like she cared.

"She apologized."

No way. This was Rachel doing damage control. Would Rachel *ever* see Suze for who she really was? "I don't believe you."

"She did!" Rachel insisted. "Said she was really sorry she laughed and stuff."

Erin was sorry too. Sorry she'd gone to the party in the first place. Sorry Zach drank beer. "Why is she apologizing to you and not to me then? It was me she laughed at." Erin slowed; they were almost at the office.

Rachel dropped her voice. "She's jealous of you. She knows Zach likes you and she knows you guys have dogs in common. She feels threatened. That's why she's so mean to you. You should feel sorry for her, not judge her."

Sorry for Suze Shillington? Yeah, right. So much for Rachel standing up for her. Things hadn't changed. Rachel was still under Suze's spell.

"She's brainwashed you, Rachel."

Rachel's blue eyes flashed. "No, she hasn't."

"She's evil."

She gave a snort of laughter. "Oh, puleese."

"Besides," Erin said, "I won't go out with a guy who drinks." *Or a guy who wasn't honest with the principal. Or told parents what he thought they wanted to hear.*

"Remember what I said last night? Zach hardly ever drinks. He's one of the good guys. I don't know what was up with him. Maybe he's worried about the CheeseBarkers competition or something."

She could relate to that, Erin decided a minute later when she saw Zach sitting in Mr. Ratzka's office. And it was true: Zach *was* one of the good guys. He was also a walking advertisement for Hot Guys Inc., even with his messy hair and wrinkled denim shirt.

He nodded in her direction. "Hey."

"Hey." Talk about hot, she felt her face flame right down to her neck.

"Come in, Erin." Mr. Ratzka gestured to a chair. "Sit down."

Erin sat.

"There's been another theft from Mr. Ponchet's room. This time it was an antique fountain pen that belonged to Mr. Ponchet's grandmother." Mr. Ratzka ran a weary hand over his balding head. "As far as we can tell, it went missing sometime between Thursday and Sunday. Zach says you and Deryk Latham were the only two in Mr. Ponchet's room Thursday and Friday, is that right?"

"Yes. But Sunday there was a group of us." She looked at Zach; he wouldn't meet her eyes. When she glanced back at Mr. Ratzka, he was studying her intently. And Erin knew exactly what he was thinking. She turned cold with fear.

"I didn't take it." Her mouth was so dry she could hardly formulate the words. "I didn't take anything."

Mr. Ratzka rested his elbows on his desk and brought his hands together. "As Zach pointed out, you and Deryk Latham have consistently been on sight whenever anything has gone missing."

Blood rushed to Erin's head. Suze had been there too. Why hadn't Zach mentioned her? "It wasn't me," she insisted. A quick glance at Zach told her he believed her. That left only one person. "And it wasn't Deryk either." Instinctively, she knew

Deryk wasn't the Carson Heights thief. "I would have seen something."

"And you didn't?"

"Nothing!"

Mr. Ratzka looked skeptical. "Well, from now on all classrooms will be locked before and after school, as well as at lunch. If either of you want access, you'll have to come to me to get the key, is that understood?"

"Yes, sir," Zach said.

"Yes, sir," Erin repeated. It didn't matter anyway. She had finished training Cupid now.

Outside the office, Erin hesitated. There was nobody around. She and Zach were alone. It was an opportunity she couldn't pass up, no matter how embarrassed she felt.

"Zach?"

"Yeah?" His skin was pale, his eyes puffy.

"I...uh...I'm sorry about last night. About...Lola." Cupid wandered out of the office and headed over to sniff the floor under the water fountain. "It was a stupid joke. I should have told you way earlier."

"No big deal." His smile looked forced. "My mom was a little choked but she'll get over it."

One down, one to go. "And, Zach, I didn't take the fountain pen. You have to believe me."

"I believe you." This time his smile reached

those gold-flecked brown eyes. "Deryk Latham, on the other hand—"

"He didn't take anything either."

"Whatever." His shrug was careless, disbelieving. "But you're no thief, Erin. Everybody knows that."

By lunchtime, however, Erin realized Zach Cameron was wrong.

Held up in social studies, Erin got to the cafeteria late. She took her place in line. A familiar laugh rang out. Erin peered around the boy in front of her. It was Suze Shillington. Was Rachel part of the group? Erin's gaze skipped over the bodies. No. But Zach was. And so were Steve and Madison.

"I don't know about that, Zach." Suze's high-pitched voice floated clearly down the line. "How can you trust her? She's walking around with an imaginary friend named Lola. Hey, for all you know, maybe Lola is the Carson Heights thief."

Their laughter killed Erin's appetite. Fighting back tears, she bolted for the privacy of the library.

———————————— •⬭——

Erin kept a low profile for the rest of the week. She got to school late; she left as soon as she could. At lunch she took Cupid up the hill to the rocky outcrop. Cupid loved chasing the squirrels. And with the warmer weather, the wild bluebells were in bloom.

Rachel joined them a few times. Suze was never discussed, although Erin knew her friend still hung around with her crowd.

Thursday, Erin had algebra last block.

"Erin," Ms. Carter called after the bell rang and they were filing out. "Can you stay behind, please? And have your notebook handy."

That didn't sound good. Erin pulled her notebook out and waited for the class to empty.

"I have your test here." Ms. Carter was perched on the edge of her desk, a stylish loafer dangling from her slim foot. "You didn't do very well."

Erin flushed. The kids called Ms. Carter the cheerleader. Not only was she young, blonde, and Barbie-beautiful, she cheered you on no matter what you did. Or how badly you did it. "What did I get?"

"Two out of forty."

What? She'd expected a low mark, but not *that* low. Her parents were going to kill her.

"Were you having an off day?" she asked softly. "Or was it the material?"

"Every day's an off day when it comes to algebra," Erin confessed. "I think I've got it, but then I get all confused." Tears clogged her throat. Her parents were going to insist she quit her job at the SPCA. And that was the last thing she wanted.

"If you can stay this afternoon and come in early tomorrow, I'll work with you and see where you're going wrong," Ms. Carter offered. "Algebra may never be your favorite subject, but you should be able to develop a working understanding of it."

Erin blinked to stop the tears from falling. "I have to be at the SPCA by five tonight, but I can stay for about an hour." Maybe her parents would be more forgiving when they found out she was putting in extra time to try and improve.

"And I'm going to let you write the test again at lunch tomorrow." She winked. "Our secret, okay?"

"Really?" Relief made Erin almost light-headed. She didn't have to tell her parents after all!

"Really." Ms. Carter smiled her picture-perfect smile. "But don't get excited. I won't give you the answers. You'll have to work for them."

And Erin did work. She worked with Ms. Carter that afternoon and on her own again that night. The SPCA was unusually quiet; she had lots of time to cram. The next morning, she was at school by seven-thirty. Ms. Carter corrected her work sheets, and though Erin still had lots wrong, she was improving. By the time she wrote the second test at lunch Friday, she felt less overwhelmed.

"I'll mark this right away," Ms. Carter promised.

"You'll have it when I give the tests back this afternoon."

Having algebra last block on Friday was never any fun, Erin reflected as she hurried through the empty halls to home ec, but at least today she could look forward to better test results.

"Erin, wait!"

Erin's blood practically stopped. It was Zach, approaching from the other direction. "I'm in a hurry," she said when he caught up. "Ms. Garrett hates it when we're late." She could hardly look at him. That whole Lola thing still embarrassed her.

"She'll understand. Ratman wants to see us."

Was it another theft? "What about?" she asked uneasily.

"I don't know."

Erin followed Zach through the office door. Cupid jumped up from his mat and waddled over as soon as he saw her. But even the sight of his ugly grin did nothing to cheer her.

"Come in, come in," Mr. Ratzka said. Erin and Zach took the two chairs in front of his desk.

"I have good news."

Good news?

"Cupid has been short-listed for the CheeseBarkers competition." He looked delighted. "Congratulations to both of you!"

Chapter Thirteen

"**W**HAT?" Zach said.

"Really?" Erin was stunned. Cupid had made the *short list*?

Mr. Ratzka's smile stretched across his face. "Cupid will compete in the CheeseBarkers competition."

Cupid had been short-listed! "That's *great*!" Erin said. "I mean, I hoped he might and I knew there was a chance, but I didn't want to get too excited." Because really, in her heart of hearts, she had expected Cupid to be eliminated.

"But it's only been a week since we sent in the video," Zach said.

Who cared? If Cupid had made the short list, he could win. He really could. She could see it now.

The New Face of CheeseBarkers is Cupid from Carson Heights Junior High. Caden Vaughan presents the $5,000 prize. Their school appears in the latest Tawp Dawg video. And Cupid's trainer is...Erin Morris!

"Apparently only a few of the entries stood out, and it didn't take them long to make their decision," Mr. Ratzka said.

Erin snapped back to attention.

Zach looked shocked. "It happened so fast."

Why wasn't he more excited? She was so excited she felt like she might lift off and float away any second.

"Everything has happened fast," Mr. Ratzka said. "And the pace won't let up any time soon. The CheeseBarkers people have decided to move the competition up. They're holding it at the downtown Hyatt Pacific a week from Wednesday."

That wasn't even two weeks away! Erin fought back panic. The judges liked what they saw; otherwise they wouldn't have short-listed him.

"Cupid knows the new song. He's practically trained, right, Zach?"

Zach nodded.

"I mean, we'll have to keep training because his jumps are weak and he won't do the slide. So I'm using the spin and the dead dog pose instead, plus I need to get him used to people because he hates crowds, but it's doable." Erin knew she was babbling, but she couldn't help herself. They were in the running for $5,000! "It's all doable." Anything was doable if you worked at it.

"Good." Mr. Ratzka reached for a notepad. "I'll

write you both notes so you don't get detentions for being late to class." He scribbled on a piece of paper. "And since it's Friday afternoon and this is a really big deal, I won't wait until the end of the day to make the announcement. I'll interrupt classes and make it now." He handed them each a slip of paper and grinned. "Congratulations!" he said again.

Erin was halfway to class when Mr. Ratzka came on the PA system. The cheer that followed was so loud she imagined the school walls shook. Everybody was still laughing and talking about it when she got to home ec.

"This is the best news ever!" Rachel shrieked before grabbing her in a bear hug. She whispered in Erin's ear: "Zach's gonna ask you to the dance for sure now!"

People crowded around, slapping her on the back, squeezing her arm.

"Way to go, Erin!"

"Congratulations, Morris."

"Five thousand dollars, here we come!"

"All right people, that's enough." Ms. Garrett clapped her hands together. "Let's get those muffins in the oven." But she smiled and when things were quiet, she came over and gave Erin's shoulder a squeeze. "Good job, Erin!"

Just before class ended, Erin found herself alone

at the washing-machine station with Deryk Latham.

"Isn't it great?" Erin said as she measured soap for the machine.

He handed her an armful of towels. "Great." But his crabby tone told Erin he really didn't think so.

First Zach was less than thrilled, and now Deryk. Erin didn't get it. "I thought you'd be happy." She stuffed the dirty linen into the washing machine and turned the dial. "What's your problem?"

Deryk scowled. "Zach Cameron's my problem, that's what."

Zach and Deryk were fighting *again*? They couldn't afford to fight. Not now. But before she could ask Deryk to explain, he stormed away.

The disappointment Erin felt over both Zach and Deryk's reaction to the news was swept aside during algebra class. Even her euphoria over Cupid's win dissolved.

She'd gotten fourteen out of forty on her algebra test. After studying long and hard, and writing the test twice, she'd still failed.

This was big-time bad.

What could she tell her parents? She needed to get home and figure it out. But leaving quickly after school proved to be difficult. People were still excited about Cupid's win, still thrilled at the possibility of winning $5,000. It took Erin more than fifteen minutes to get to her locker and grab what she needed for the weekend.

Rachel appeared by her side as Erin slammed her locker door. "What's with you?"

"What do you mean?" Suze and Zach were heading their way.

"You were so excited when you got the news." Rachel's brown eyes studied her carefully. "What happened?"

She wouldn't confide in Rachel with Suze and Zach nearby. "Nothing, don't worry about it."

"We did it!" Suze said when she joined them. "We got Cupid short-listed!" She was preening like a self-possessed cat.

"Way to go, Erin." Zach looked happier now. How ironic. He was feeling better and she was feeling worse. "I didn't get a chance to congratulate you earlier. You did a great job training Cupid."

"And *I* did a great job writing the letter and editing the video." Suze batted her massively long eyelashes in Zach's direction.

"An awesome job," Rachel agreed.

Erin shrugged on her sweater and started walking. How could she break the news about the test to her parents?

Zach fell into step beside her. "You realize what this means?"

"What?" Rachel and Suze trailed behind; Erin heard them giggling softly.

"It means Cupid's gonna win!" Zach said as they approached the front door of the school. "And Carson Heights is gonna end up $5,000 richer."

Unease prickled the back of Erin's neck. She thought Cupid would win too. But what if he didn't?

"You're the only one who could have trained him." Zach opened the door for her. "We owe this success to you."

We owe this success to you. The unease flared into a tight, hard knot.

"You could end up being a dog whisperer *and* a hero," Suze added as they stopped walking.

Rachel frowned. "Be nice."

"I *am* being nice." Suze flipped her long black hair over her shoulder and smiled at Erin. "You win Carson Heights the money and a spot in the Tawp Dawg video, and you'll be a real hero. Even I can appreciate that."

It was the first truly nice thing Suze had ever said to her. But what really stunned her was the look in Suze's eyes. It was suspiciously close to admiration. Did Suze really think if Cupid won, she'd be a hero?

Like, no pressure.

"I've gotta go," Erin mumbled when she finally found her voice. "I'll see you guys Monday."

———————————— • ⬯

Erin went home, retrieved Blue, and walked over to the ravine in Mahon Park. Blue ambled beside the gurgling creek, sniffed rocks and tree stumps, did the occasional three-legged sprint after a sparrow. The seclusion gave Erin time to think.

Her parents had been clear—if she didn't get her algebra mark up, she had to quit the SPCA. And she *couldn't* quit, not when she was this close to getting a paid position.

Then there was Cupid. Now that he'd made the short list, he needed more training. But her parents were going to make her cut back on all her extracurricular activities. Including training Cupid.

You win Carson Heights the money and you'll be a true hero.

Suze Shillington had really said that, Erin recalled as Blue came to a sudden stop by a fallen log. *A true hero.*

Blue's tail went up. His head went down. He pawed excitedly at the ground. Erin couldn't help but grin at his enthusiasm. Even with three legs, he was still the most beautiful dog she'd ever seen.

There was no guarantee Cupid would win the CheeseBarkers competition, Erin reflected as she walked home. There were four other dogs in the running. How would people treat her if Cupid lost?

How would Suze Shillington treat her?

Erin avoided her parents until dinner. Finally, as her dad dished out chicken stir-fry, she told them about her mark.

"Fourteen out of forty is pretty bad," her mother agreed as she finished pouring the water and sat down.

Two out of forty was even worse, but Erin wasn't about to tell them she'd written the test twice!

Dad passed the rice. "Don't look so miserable, bug-face. There are worse things in life than failing an algebra test."

Yeah, like having to leave the SPCA. And letting her school down.

Erin stared at the colorful medley of food on her plate. She usually loved the ginger-onion tang of Chinese food, but tonight she didn't feel like eating. "You said if I failed the test I had to quit the SPCA and cut back on my extracurricular activities."

"I did say that, didn't I?" Mom admitted.

Erin nodded and pushed a carrot around her plate. She'd really miss the dogs. Man, she didn't want to give it up. Furiously, she speared some chicken.

"Your mother might have been too hasty," Dad said. "Cupid's training is over and there can't be that many more strings sessions left. But you do need to spend more time on algebra. What if you gave up your extra shift at the SPCA and went back to Saturdays only?"

"That's a good compromise," her mother said.

It could have been worse. They could have insisted she quit. But what about Cupid?

"We think we're being reasonable," her father finally said. "What's the problem?"

Her life was the problem. "Cupid made the short list today." Erin toyed with a small mound of brown rice. "He might become the new face of CheeseBarkers."

A broad grin split her father's face. "Congratulations!"

"That's wonderful, darling!"

"I guess."

Her mother's fork paused midway to her mouth. "You don't seem happy about it."

"You said I had to cut down on my extracurricular stuff. Cupid still needs a lot of training if he's gonna win."

Her parents exchanged glances. "Oh," her mother said.

"How much training?" her father asked.

"Every day for the next eleven days."

"Is there anyone else who could work with him?"

Dad didn't understand how training dogs worked. "Cupid answers to me," Erin explained. "It would be hard getting him used to someone else at this stage. Besides, I'm the one they saw on the video."

"And training Cupid is something you really want to do?" Mom probed.

Did she? Suze's words spooled out in her head. *You'll be a dog whisperer and a hero.*

"Rachel roped you into this at the start," Mom reminded her. "Do you want to continue?"

Here was her opportunity. She could tell her parents no, let them forbid her from working with Cupid, and have the perfect opportunity to wiggle out from her problem. But if she backed out, she'd let the school down.

On the other hand, if she tried and Cupid lost, she'd let the school down too.

She was in a no-win situation.

"Let's get you a math tutor," Dad said. At Erin's look of disgust, he held up his hand. "I know we talked about it before and you don't like the idea, but if it's going to bring up your algebra mark and allow you to continue on with Cupid, I think it's a good idea."

"I agree," Mom said. "A number of my students have tutors and they only put in about half an hour before school a few times a week. I'm sure I could find someone for you. How about it, Erin?"

"I guess."

Her father studied her thoughtfully. "What's really bothering you, bug-face? It's not the math tutor, is it?"

Wordlessly, Erin shook her head. It was a full minute before she trusted herself to speak. "It wasn't such a big deal when we first entered Cupid in the contest. People didn't think he stood a chance. And I did my best training him, but nobody expected him to make the finals."

A lone tear snaked its way down her cheek; Erin wiped it away. "But now that he has, people expect him to win for sure. They were coming up to me in the halls today as if Carson Heights has already *won* the $5,000. They keep going on about how much fun it's gonna be to appear in the Tawp Dawg video." Erin paused and took a breath.

"What if I fail?" she whispered. "What if I lose the school $5,000?" Just saying the words out loud made her nauseous. "I'll be responsible."

"No, you won't," Dad said.

"All you can do is your best," Mom added. "You have no control over the outcome."

Erin knew that. She'd also been to enough dog

shows to know you could never predict how they would turn out. But that didn't make her feel any better. "Cupid doesn't take orders well," she reminded them. "And he doesn't like performing in front of people. It was practically impossible to get him on video."

"Being afraid to fail is no reason to avoid a challenge," her father pointed out.

We owe this success to you. Zach's words echoed through her mind. Cupid was used to her. No one could take her place at this point. If she left, they'd have to pull Cupid from the competition. And that wasn't fair to the school either. She had to go ahead.

"We're meeting you halfway on the mark situation," Dad reminded her. "You can keep your position at the SPCA if you cut back to Saturdays until your mark comes back up. And you can train Cupid if you get a math tutor. Okay?"

It wasn't okay. She didn't want to cut back a shift at the SPCA, she didn't want a tutor, and she really didn't want to risk Cupid blowing the competition. But she had no choice.

Mom smiled. "We believe in you, Erin. We know you'll give it your best shot."

"Right." And she would. Of course she would.

But would her best shot be good enough?

Chapter Fourteen

MONDAY MORNING, North Vancouver was in the middle of a spring downpour. Stepping into the school foyer, Erin snapped her bright yellow umbrella shut and shook the droplets of water onto the floor. The halls were crowded; people had come inside to get out of the rain. Erin tucked the umbrella under her arm and headed for the west wing. She was late, not watching where she was going. She took the corner too quickly and almost barreled into Deryk and Zach.

"You're a fraud, Cameron, that's what you are." Deryk poked his finger into Zach's chest.

"Don't touch me, Latham!" Zach pushed Deryk's hand away. "And you're overreacting. I am not a fraud."

"Oh yeah?" Deryk sneered. "Then that girlfriend of yours is."

Girlfriend? A tiny choking sound escaped from Erin's throat. He meant Suze.

That's when the boys noticed her.

"Perfect timing," Deryk said. An expression Erin didn't recognize crossed his face. He turned back to Zach. "Why don't you tell her how you and Suze cheated on the video."

Zach's face turned the color of beet soup.

Cheated on the video? With Suze?

"Or were you going to keep it a secret?" Deryk jeered. "And let her find out at the CheeseBarkers competition?" With one final look of disgust, he turned on his heel and walked away.

He doesn't need to learn the whole routine. An icy chill snaked its way down Erin's back. *We can always fake the rest.* "What does he mean you cheated?"

"I...just a bit of creative editing, that's all."

Something sucked the air out of Erin's lungs. Was that why Deryk had been less than thrilled when Cupid had been short-listed? "Creative editing, how?"

Zach pulled her away from the center of the hall to the alcove by the water fountain. Students rushed past, laughing and chattering about what they did on the weekend, about their upcoming classes. The sound was like a distant wind; Erin hardly noticed it. "Did you fake something?" she asked.

"No way!" Zach leaned against the wall and gave

her a killer smile. "We just used the slide move Cupid did that one time, remember?"

She remembered all right. Because Cupid hated doing it. "I cut that move out. He ends on the spin and dead dog pose. You know that."

"Yeah, but like Suze said, the slide move was cute so we edited it in."

Suze again. "That's cheating."

"Not really."

"Yes it is. The video you sent in is misleading."

"No, it's not." When he leaned close to whisper in her ear, Erin caught a whiff of his citrus lime cologne. "No more misleading than faking up a mute friend." He chuckled.

Erin's heart trampolined in her chest. There was a huge difference between making up Lola to impress Zach and making the judges think Cupid could do a slide move. *Wasn't* there?

"Look," he said. "If you can teach Cupid to do the slide in a week, great. If not, just end like you planned. It's no big deal." The smell of Zach's cologne was making Erin queasy; she took a step back. "The CheeseBarkers people aren't going to expect Cupid's routine to be exactly as it is on the video anyway."

Zach had a point. Dog routines varied a little bit

every time the animal did them. That was a given. But this felt like a big deal. "I don't know," Erin said. "It feels like we're cheating."

"You worry too much." Zach dropped an arm on her shoulder and propelled her down the hall. Once upon a time, the feel of his body bumping into hers would have been enough to send her into orbit. Now all she felt was confused. Was she overreacting?

"We've got a copy of the final video on the computer," Zach said. "Watch it at lunch. It's no big deal. The slide went into the routine like it was meant to be. Suze was right about that." He grinned again and disappeared down the hall.

Erin sipped her milk and tried to swallow the chunk of ham and cheese sandwich lodged in her throat. The video played on the computer screen in front of her. Not only had Suze edited in the slide move, but she'd added a tiny flick of Cupid's paw that made it look like he was saluting as the "Feed me Luv" chorus ended.

How could Zach have agreed to it? Especially after she'd told him she didn't want to fake anything.

It was Suze. *She* had convinced him. She could charm the rattles off a rattlesnake. He was under Suze's spell. Just like Rachel was.

"It certainly makes Cupid stand out," Rachel said, peering over Erin's shoulder and munching a carrot stick.

Mona sat on her right, eating a tuna salad wrap. "It's not so bad. The judges won't *necessarily* expect Cupid to salute."

"Unless Suze mentioned the salute in the letter," Deryk muttered.

Erin had cornered Deryk in foods class. He'd admitted hearing Suze and Zach talking about the video the day before Cupid had been short-listed. It was obvious from the conversation that Suze had done some creative editing. When Erin had asked Deryk why he hadn't told anyone, he'd scowled and mumbled something about not being a gossip. Besides, he'd added, he hadn't seen the video and didn't know how bad it was. And he hadn't expected it to matter anyway.

In other words, he hadn't expected Cupid to make the short list. But before Erin could challenge him on *that*, he'd suggested they meet in the computer lab at lunch. He knew where Suze had stored the master copy of the video; he could pull it up on the computer. Erin had made him promise to come alone and not tell anyone. She'd also sworn Rachel and Mona to secrecy.

Now, disgust flickered in Deryk's pale blue eyes. "Cameron and Shillington should have run the video by you before they submitted it."

A gust of wind sent rain splattering against the computer room window. The dark, gloomy day matched Erin's mood. Deryk was right. "Can you play it again?" she asked.

Deryk set aside his burger and cued up the video.

It was no better the second, third, or twelfth time.

"What are you going to do?" Mona asked.

"I don't know," Erin admitted.

"Cameron and Shillington should be held accountable," Deryk said. "You should complain to Ratman."

"No, she shouldn't," Rachel said. "He'll go to the people at CheeseBarkers, Cupid will be disqualified, and we won't have a shot at the $5,000."

The four of them stared at one another. *We've come this far. We're almost there.* Zach was right. There was only one choice.

"I'll try to teach Cupid the slide move," Erin said. A sense of foreboding mushroomed in her chest. "But there's nothing I can do about that salute."

"Then don't worry about it." Rachel fiddled with the gold chain around her neck. "Just do the best you can."

Just do the best you can. Easy for her to say.

The loud peel of a bell interrupted them.

"That's the fire alarm," Mona said.

They jumped from their seats and hurried to the door. In the corridor, students and staff headed swiftly for the exit at the end of the hall. "This better be for real," someone complained as they filed into the rain. "There's no way I want to stand around in this weather just for a drill."

Amen to that, Erin thought, following the others to the rain-slicked asphalt of the basketball court.

"Hey, Erin!" Zach called as he passed under the basketball hoop and headed in her direction. He was followed by Suze, Madison, and Steve.

Erin studied the two of them carefully. Suze gazed up at him adoringly; Zach didn't seem to notice. But he was clearly under her spell. The question was, *how* committed were they to each other?

"I'm glad I caught you," he said when he reached her side. Even with rain dripping down his forehead, he was still the hottest-looking guy at Carson Heights. "I know you want to see the video and I couldn't find you in the cafeteria."

She and Mona exchanged glances. "I've already seen it."

Zach looked surprised. "You did?"

A drop of rain ran down his cheek to the corner of his mouth. Erin resisted the urge to reach out and brush it away. Instead she pushed her own hair back from her face and wondered if her mascara was running. "Yeah, I did."

"Wasn't it fabulous?" Suze beamed. "Didn't I do a great job on the editing?"

"I've gotta go," Deryk muttered. He stomped away.

"It was great, wasn't it?" Suze demanded again.

"Just great," Erin said coolly. "Thanks." *For nothing.*

Rachel shot her a warning glance. She always could read Erin's mind.

Mona glanced uneasily from Erin to Suze. "I'll talk to you later." As she went off to join Lesley and Jocelyn, Zach fell into a discussion about soccer with Steve.

"You know, I've been thinking about your clothes." Suze's appraising glance lingered on Erin's beige sweater, her faded corduroys. "What you can wear to show Cupid to the best advantage."

Erin braced herself for another insult. Instead Suze surprised her.

"I have a few things in my closet that might work," the other girl offered. "You're taller than me, but I have some pants that I've practically never worn and I'm sure they'd fit." Her gaze settled on Erin's hips and thighs. "Plus, I have this amazing silk top my mom brought back from Montreal last year and it would look great against your black hair."

The top probably looked like a rag, Erin thought.

Rachel broke the silence. "That would be great, right, Erin?" Her brown eyes held an unspoken plea. *Try to get along*, they said.

"I...I guess." Erin didn't want to borrow any of Suze's clothes.

"Why don't you come over tonight and try some stuff on?" She turned to Rachel and Madison. "You too. We'll make it a party."

A party? Visions of hot tubs and alcohol swam through Erin's mind. That was followed by a vision of the video Suze had ruined. "Not tonight," she said quickly. "I'm busy."

"After school, then," Suze said. "I'll order pizza."

She didn't want to go to Suze's house. Not again. She put her off a second time. "I have to train Cupid after school today."

The alarm bell came to a sudden stop. "All clear!" Mr. Ratzka yelled to the crowd.

Slowly people filed back into the school. Suze linked her arm through Erin's like they were new best friends. "So Ratman says Carson Heights can send a delegation of ten to the competition," she said.

A delegation? This was news.

"Only ten?" Madison wrinkled her nose. "That's not many."

"No kidding," Suze agreed. "Especially when you consider that Erin, Zach, and Deryk have to be there because they've done the most work. That only leaves seven others."

"Five," Erin interjected. "Mona has been a big help. I want her there. And Rachel too."

As they reached the doors, Miss Pickering rushed out, Cupid in her arms, a wild look in her eyes.

"It's all over," Erin told her. "It was a false alarm."

The secretary put her hand over her heart. "Thank goodness. I couldn't find Cupid for the longest time!"

Erin reached out and gave the bulldog's head a scratch as they walked into the building.

"They should tie that dog up," Suze said under her breath.

Erin eased her arm away from Suze, but the other girl moved closer. "About that delegation," she said. "Ratman's going to ask you for a list of names. I'd sure like it if you'd put me on the list."

"Me too!" Madison squealed.

So that was it. Suze was willing to loan her clothes so she'd be included in the delegation. But loaning clothes didn't make up for all those months of being mean.

"That won't be a problem, will it, Erin?" When Erin didn't answer, Rachel rushed on. "I mean, Suze wrote the letter and edited the video, and now she's gonna loan you her clothes. She should be included. Madison too."

"It's not just up to me," Erin said as they reached the foyer. "It's up to Zach too."

"Zach will go along with whatever we want," Suze said carelessly. "He always does."

Was Zach that easily led? As Erin digested that, Madison added, "Zach's the most easygoing guy at Carson Heights."

"I'll talk to him," Erin said.

"Well, my offer still stands," Suze lifted her wet hair from the back of her neck and twisted it into a messy knot. "Come over after school any day this week. Except Wednesday when I have cheerleading practice. But any other day is good."

"I'll see." Erin was noncommittal.

"Stay for dinner. We'll get pizza. Or Chinese. Whatever you want," Suze offered generously.

Erin recognized the hint of desperation in the

other girl's eyes. She knew exactly what it was like to be on the outside looking in, never knowing if you'd be included. For the first time all year, Erin was in the middle of the action and Suze wasn't. It was pretty heady stuff.

"I'll see," she repeated.

"I've made an effort to get to know Mona," Rachel said when they were alone. "The least you could do is make an effort to get to know Suze!"

Erin rolled her eyes. "Mona didn't wreck the video. Suze did, remember? Besides, she's only being nice because she wants to be part of the delegation."

"Of course she wants to be part of it," Rachel said, "but that's not the only thing. She wants to be your friend. I've told you that before. And as for the video, her heart was in the right place. She wants Carson Heights to win, that's all."

Erin didn't respond. Rachel had looked at the bright side of things for so long she was blind to Suze's dark side.

"Just try," Rachel urged. "She really wants to be your friend. Why can't you accept that?"

Maybe Rachel was right. Maybe she was wrong. Maybe she'd underestimated Suze Shillington all these months. Maybe she really did want to be her friend.

And maybe pigs could fly.

Chapter Fifteen

"I'M NOT SURE I UNDERSTAND." Erin stared at Mr. Ratzka. The long, low window in his office let in a warm blanket of noon-hour sun, which was a welcome relief after yesterday's heavy rain. "Are you saying I can't train Cupid at all anymore?"

"I'm saying I don't want you training Cupid at school anymore," Mr. Ratzka clarified. "This last theft has left us no choice."

Now a cell phone was missing from the computer lab. It was theft number six. Mr. Ratzka thought she had taken it. She could tell by the look in his eyes. No question, it looked bad. She and Deryk and Mona and Rachel had been the last ones to use the room. But there'd been that fire drill, and no time to lock up. Someone could have taken the phone when they were outside.

Someone did. Because she certainly hadn't. "Can you call the cell phone number and trace it?" she asked.

"We tried, and so did the phone company. They got no signal."

"I didn't take it!" Her voice trembled. "I wouldn't be telling you to trace the phone if I did."

Sighing, he leaned back in his chair. "I don't know what to think. You're a responsible girl, Erin. All your teachers say so. And you've never been in trouble before, but..." His voice trailed away.

But she'd been there every single time something had gone missing. The unspoken words hung in the air between them like a giant elephant. And like a giant elephant they threatened to suffocate her.

If it wasn't her, then who was it?

"We're going into total lockdown before, during, and after school," Mr. Ratzka told her. "Only teachers will have access to their classrooms and to the extracurricular rooms. There will be no exceptions made until we get to the bottom of this."

Before she fled, Erin mumbled something about understanding and being sorry. She wasn't sure what she should be sorry for, but somehow she felt guilty sitting across that wide oak conference table while he studied her like she was a lowlife criminal.

The guilty feeling persisted for the rest of the afternoon.

Kids were talking about her. Erin could tell. The

moment she walked into social studies, an awkward silence fell. Same thing happened in home ec. Algebra was even worse. When Erin slid into her seat, Cynthia made a crack about nailing down her backpack. Half the class broke into laughter.

She didn't need that kind of grief on top of training Cupid.

And working on Cupid's routine had to be her priority. The competition was next week; there was no time to waste. Thankfully, Miss Pickering agreed to let them use her basement. Obviously she didn't consider Erin a thief.

Erin and Mona took Cupid to Miss Pickering's house Tuesday at lunch. They still couldn't get him to do the slide, and he wouldn't repeat that funny little salute Suze had included, but he had the rest of the routine down.

"Why the long face?" Rachel asked after school Tuesday.

"Mona can't stay after school to practice," Erin said. The contest was a week tomorrow; they had to get as many practice sessions in as they could.

"Good."

"Good?" Had Rachel lost her mind? "What's good about it?"

"Now you can come to Suze's place. Come on, Erin, make an effort!"

Suze appeared at the end of the hall; Rachel waved her over. "Erin's free this afternoon," she said before Erin could speak. "How about we do the clothes and pizza thing?"

"Great idea!"

There was nothing great about it, Erin decided an hour later when she was stripped down to her underwear in Suze's bedroom. If Rachel hadn't begged, she never would have come. And she wouldn't be standing in front of Suze's mirror wearing her oldest bra and panties and feeling like a fool.

"Here, try these." Suze pitched another pair of pants in Erin's direction.

She caught them but made no move to put them on. Erin didn't obsess about clothes, although she knew it was important to look good in the show ring. But lately she had more important things on her mind. Like getting Cupid to do the slide move. Not blowing the contest. And proving she wasn't the Carson Heights thief.

"Come on, Erin." Rachel and Madison were curled up in a cocoon of cushions in the center of Suze's king-size bed. "We're waiting."

Erin eyed the tag in the back of the pants. Size zero. "I don't think they'll fit."

Suze looked over, quirked her eyebrow. "Of course they'll fit, silly. You're not *that* fat." She turned back to her cupboard.

You're not that fat.

It didn't sound like an insult, so why did it feel like one? She glanced at Rachel, but her friend had grabbed the remote control and was busy searching for something interesting to watch on Suze's huge, flat-screen television.

Erin slid her feet into the trendy jeans, eased them up her calves, stopped just past her knees. No way would these would go over her thighs. Just like all the others hadn't.

Sighing, she slipped them off and stared at the pile on Suze's fluffy white rug. Shirts, sweaters, pants, and shoes. More stuff than Erin had owned in her entire life.

"No?" Suze asked, turning around.

"No."

"We have to find you something. You need to look good, right? "

Right. So why was Suze handing her a pile of stuff that didn't fit and made her feel like a fat cow? Because she wanted to get on the delegation list.

And if she made Erin feel fat in the process, that was okay, too.

Suze handed her another pair. "Try these." She disappeared into the closet again.

At least she could get these ones all the way up her legs. And if she sucked her stomach all the way back to her spine she could do them up too.

"They fit!" Suze exclaimed when she glimpsed Erin in the mirror. "Look, guys, we found a pair that work!" She clapped her hands and for a minute Erin thought her smile might actually be genuine. Then she remembered: this was Suze Shillington she was dealing with.

Rachel threw down the remote and Madison tossed aside her magazine. Erin felt like a stuffed sausage about to pop.

"They only fit if I don't breathe when I'm wearing them." She lowered the zipper, let out her stomach. Immediate relief.

The three girls gave a collective sigh of disappointment.

"Well, I don't have anything that's a bigger size," Suze said flatly. "I guess your own pants will have to do. At least the silk top fits. You may as well keep it. It's huge on me."

"When are we getting pizza?" Madison asked. "I'm hungry."

While they waited for the pizza delivery, Suze offered to shape Erin's eyebrows. "I'm fine, thanks." They were sprawled out on Suze's deck, drinking pink lemonade. Erin had deliberately turned her chair away from the hot tub. Staring at it reminded her of Suze's party. Of Zach drinking.

Zach's the most easygoing guy at Carson Heights. Was that why he'd been drinking? To impress Suze? Rachel didn't think they were going out, and neither did Mona, but Erin wasn't so sure. And she wasn't leaving Suze's house until she found out what was up with them. Zach was one of the good guys, even Rachel had said so. Erin still wanted to date him. And if they went out, he sure wouldn't drink. She'd influence him for the better.

"I don't like to say anything but your eyebrows could really use work." Suze smiled.

No matter how nice Suze was being, she'd have to be dead before she'd let Suze anywhere near her face. Besides, her eyebrows were fine. She'd learned how to pluck them last summer when her friends Cassie and Treena had given her a makeover. Or, as they liked to call it, a reinvention. "They're fine," she said again as she sipped her lemonade

Suze's gaze dropped to Erin's hands. "How about your nails then? I do a mean manicure?"

She was so *not* the manicure type, Erin thought. And Rachel knew it because she immediately jumped to Erin's defense. "The pizza will be here soon. Let's do the poll in Madison's magazine instead."

"What poll?"

Madison grabbed the magazine off the deck and began flipping pages. "The one about what girls like in guys."

Now that sounded like a great way to bring the conversation around to Zach. She had to know whether she still stood a chance with him.

"I like a guy who stands about five-foot-eleven with dark hair and an Italian background," Rachel said.

They all laughed. It was Anthony to a T. "You're not supposed to describe your boyfriend, silly." Suze snatched the magazine out of Madison's hand and skimmed the list. "You're supposed to submit the top three qualities you like in a guy. They'll publish the results two months from now." She tossed the magazine back down. "Let's see," she murmured, staring into space. "He has to look good in jeans. That's a given."

Zach looked amazing in jeans, Erin thought.

"And he should be a risk taker too," she added.

Was that how she talked Zach into going along with her editing job? And drinking the beer? Told him he should take a risk? Zach, being so easygoing, would have agreed.

"Personally, I like a guy with a nice smile. And it helps if he has money." Madison laughed.

Rachel rolled her eyes. "How *you*, Madison."

Madison took Rachel's teasing with a good-natured grin. She was the first to admit she had the most expensive taste of any girl on the planet.

"I like a guy with brains," Rachel mused. "And a good sense of humor." She turned to Erin. "How about you?"

Erin hesitated. She wanted all those things in a guy too: brains, a sense of humor, a nice smile, a good body. But truthfully, there were other things she cared more about. If she said anything, they'd tease her for sure. And that would make her feel like such a loser.

"Come on, Erin," Suze pressed. "Tell us your list."

On the other hand, she wasn't going to lie. Not anymore. She took a breath. "He has to be honest. And kind," she added quickly. "Not in a fake-it-up way, but really, truly, *caring* kind." The three girls stared at her. "And he has to have nice eyes," she said as an afterthought.

"You could be describing Zach," Madison teased.

Erin's face flamed. She *was* describing Zach. *We can always fake it up.* Wasn't she?

"It doesn't matter who she's describing," Suze interrupted. "Erin has a point. If the guy isn't kind, he's going to jerk you around and nobody wants that." She gave Erin an appraising look. "I'm with you on the kindness thing."

"Me too," Madison said.

Erin was shocked speechless. Suze was sincere. She could see it in her eyes.

Maybe Rachel's new crowd of friends was her crowd too.

Then Suze asked, "Blue or brown?"

Erin blinked. "Pardon?"

"Eyes. Blue or brown?" Suze demanded.

Zach had brown—actually golden brown—eyes. So why had a pair of icy blue eyes flashed into her mind first? "Brown, I guess."

The doorbell rang, breaking off the conversation. It was the pizza. As Erin followed the others down the hall, she pushed the vision of those pale blue eyes away.

They were Deryk Latham's eyes.

And they didn't belong in her head. Erin didn't get why they were there in the first place. She still didn't get it long after the pizza was finished and she was at home. And she didn't get whether Suze and Zach were dating either.

She hadn't asked. Which meant she was no closer to an answer about whether she still stood a chance with Zach Cameron or not.

Chapter Sixteen

THE NEXT FEW DAYS UNFOLDED without any more thefts. Even the cracks about Erin being the Carson Heights thief stopped. People had more important things on their minds. Like winning the CheeseBarkers competition and the fact that the boys' soccer team had made the city semifinals. That meant Zach was often tied up, and the cheerleaders were busier too. Even so, Suze came by Erin's locker every day after school to ask how the training was going. She seemed genuinely concerned when Erin told her Cupid still couldn't do the slide move. So, when Mr. Ratzka asked who she wanted in the CheeseBarkers delegation, Erin put Suze and Madison down without a second thought.

She felt like part of the gang now. Why shouldn't they be included?

"When are you going to put Cupid through the routine in front of a group?" Deryk asked as the week drew to a close and they headed to their lockers. "He has to get used to performing in front of people before the competition."

"I know," Erin said. "We need to do it soon." Deryk had gotten his hair cut. She'd swear he'd gotten streaks too. It looked good. "Ratman wants to be there. Because of the thefts and stuff. I have to check with him first."

Zach ran up, carrying his green and white soccer bag. "Erin, hey! Did you see that show on the Discovery Channel last night about teaching dogs routines?" When she told him no, he grabbed a DVD from his bag and shoved it into her hand. "I recorded it for you. Maybe there's something that'll help with Cupid." He waved. "Gotta go."

"Good luck with the game!" Erin yelled after him. She clutched the DVD to her chest. She still didn't know how serious Zach was about Suze, but she did know one thing: he still sent her heart winging up past Mars.

"What a jerk," Deryk muttered.

"Why don't you like him?" Erin asked as they reached her locker.

"My dad hired him and two other guys to help me dig the drain tiles in our front yard last summer. Zach swore he knew what do to." Deryk shook his head in disgust. "He didn't. The rest of us sweated our guts out while he stood around issuing orders and looking good."

Deryk was probably jealous. Everybody liked to look good, although Zach didn't have to try, it came naturally to him. Erin was still thinking about looks a few minutes later when she and Mona went to pick up Cupid.

They found Miss Pickering obsessing about the bulldog's jowls. "Do you think they hang down more than they used to?" The school secretary studied his chin with a worried frown.

"Not at all," Erin reassured her. Bulldogs had droopy jowls. It was the nature of the breed.

"I don't know." Miss Pickering dug through the desk drawer where she kept Cupid's leash. "I think gravity is having its way with him. It's so sad. He was such a beautiful puppy."

Erin and Mona exchanged grins. Erin didn't get it. If Miss Pickering had wanted a beautiful dog she could have gotten a Flat-Coat like Blue or even an Irish setter like Lucille. Bulldogs were meant to be ugly. Why fight it?

Friday afternoon's training session was a bit of a bust. Cupid was easily distracted, Mona's cell phone kept going off, and Erin wanted to get home and watch Zach's DVD. But when she finally watched it that night, she was disappointed. There was nothing she could use with Cupid.

Saturday morning Erin had a short shift at the SPCA—Richard had agreed to give her the afternoon off to work with Cupid—and Mona had skating. But Erin spent Saturday afternoon and all day Sunday with Cupid.

"Cupid's going to win," Erin predicted Sunday at dinner. "You should see him dance! I even got him to do the slide a couple of times." Okay, so he wasn't doing it consistently, but it *was* a start. And they still had three days until the contest.

Her dad looked up from the roast beef he was carving. "I'm glad you're so confident, Erin."

She was confident in Cupid. Confident in herself. Between them, they were going to win Carson Heights $5,000. And a spot in the Tawp Dawg video. She'd be a hero. H.E.R.O.

Her mother dished up mashed potatoes. "I'm sure your hard work had a lot to do with it."

"Maybe. But part of it is Cupid himself. I've never seen a dog take to music the way he did. And so fast too. He's a winner for sure." Erin helped herself to peas and carrots. "Everybody knows it too."

Her parents exchanged glances.

"Don't get your hopes up, bug-face." Dad put two

slices of roast beef on her plate. "Be happy with a job well done. Don't expect a certain outcome. Expectations have a way of letting you down."

Blue's tail thumped softly on the mat by the sink. Erin glanced over and grinned. He smelled the roast beef and expected after-dinner treats.

"You expected Blue to win the nomination," Mom reminded her gently. "You wanted him to be the face for disabled dogs. And you were terribly let down. We don't want you to be disappointed, that's all."

"Don't worry." Erin sliced into her beef. "I'm not going to be disappointed this time."

Cupid had to win. He *would* win. Erin refused to believe otherwise.

Monday afternoon all hell broke loose.

It started with an innocent knock on the door of algebra class. Mr. Ratzka poked his head through the doorway. "Is Cupid here?"

"No," Ms. Carter said.

Mr. Ratzka's eyes lingered on Erin and Mona. Erin forced herself not to squirm. Every time he looked at her these days, she felt guilty. She shouldn't, but she did. "You girls haven't seen him?" he asked.

"Not since lunch."

She and Mona had taken Cupid to Miss

Pickering's for a quick training session, but they'd returned him to the office long before the bell rang.

Frowning, Mr. Ratzka disappeared into the hall. After exchanging uneasy glances, Erin and Mona returned to their work.

Mr. Ratzka made an announcement over the public address system less than an hour later.

"Excuse the interruption, but we cannot locate Cupid. Would everyone please check their classrooms, and then send one person down to the office to report in. Thank you."

"He's probably hiding behind the fridge in the cafeteria or something," Mona murmured to Erin as they began searching. It didn't take long to confirm what they already knew. Cupid wasn't inside the math room.

Half a dozen kids were already in the office when Erin arrived. Several more hurried through the door while she talked to Mr. Ratzka. One look at their faces told the story: no one had found Cupid.

"It's my fault!" Miss Pickering sat in the corner, fiddling with the large cameo pin on her blouse. "The carpenters were repairing Mr. Ponchet's roof and Cupid hated the banging. He was so restless this morning, I should have asked you girls to leave him at home after the training session. Now he's missing." Her voice trembled with emotion.

Missing? Cupid couldn't be missing. It wasn't possible. "There has to be a logical explanation," Erin murmured.

Afternoon classes were quickly forgotten. Students broke into groups. Search parties were formed. They were instructed to pay careful attention to those areas where people ate: the cafeteria, the home-ec room, the common area off the front entrance.

When the school dismissal bell rang an hour and a half later, Erin was forced to admit the unthinkable: Cupid really *was* missing. She listened from a far-off, distant place to Mr. Ratzka's after-school announcement. "Appreciate...help. Those with time...stay behind...continue to search."

Erin considered the possibilities. There were only two. Either the bulldog was fine and he'd wandered off to satisfy some urge—probably a food-related one—or he wasn't fine at all and he was truly lost.

Something told her it was the latter. And that conclusion left her breathless.

"I'll stay behind to search," Rachel offered when they filed out of homeroom.

"Me too," Mona said.

As Erin followed them to the office a few minutes

later, it was like she was living a dream. Or rather a nightmare. Any minute now, she'd wake up and this wouldn't be real. But it was real. Surreal, was more like it. Voices filled the air around her.

"He's our ticket to $5,000."

"He's probably at Sweet Rosie's. snacking as we speak."

"There are worse things to lose."

"The CheeseBarkers contest is on the line."

Of course the contest mattered. But Cupid mattered more. Where was he? Had he been doggie-snatched? Was he hurt? Scared? Hungry?

Except Cupid was always hungry.

More than fifty kids stayed after school to look for the bulldog. They searched the classrooms again, plus the cafeteria, the home-ec room, the common area. A group of kids even canvassed the houses on either side of the school and across the street.

By five o'clock, Miss Pickering was the color of chalk and looked just as brittle. "I knew something was wrong," she said as Mr. Ratzka called the police. Her eyes were red-rimmed; her hair was tumbling out of its braid. "Cupid's never been gone this long before."

"I'm sure we'll find him," Mona said.

Most of the kids had gone home; there were less than a dozen left. How could they stand around talking? Erin wondered, eyeing Rachel and Madison chatting in the corner. Zach talked to Steve. They were probably talking about the CheeseBarkers competition. Everybody but Mona and Miss Pickering seemed more concerned about the $5,000. Erin didn't get it. Blowing the contest was nothing compared to losing Cupid.

She had to do something. Anything. She called Richard. After listening to her plight, he offered to contact the radio stations and have a missing dog announcement broadcast. "With any luck, they'll air it by five thirty," he said.

Gratified to have more help, Erin hung up the phone and stood for a minute with her hand on the receiver saying a silent prayer of thanks. Just as she turned to tell everyone what Richard was arranging, a workman appeared in the doorway. His hard hat was crooked; his face was streaked with dirt.

"Look what I found." A broad smile stretched across his face. Cupid was cradled in his arms.

Miss Pickering's eyes widened. She flew across the room, tears streaming down her cheeks. "Baby! Where *were* you?"

Whimpering, the bulldog squirmed away from the workman into Miss Pickering's outstretched hands. He licked her face as if he hadn't seen her in years. "Where *were* you?" Miss Pickering demanded again as she laughed and cried and hugged her baby. "I was so *scared*!"

Everyone crowded around the two of them. "Is he okay?" Erin asked.

"Seems okay to me," the workman said as he shook hands with Mr. Ratzka. After a minute, Cupid jumped from Miss Pickering's arms, bolted for his dish, and lapped furiously at the water. "Obviously thirsty, though." He grinned.

"Where did you find him?" Mr. Ratzka asked.

The workman's name was Doug; Erin saw the black scrolling letters printed on his overalls. "Remember the old crawl space under the school?" His eyes twinkled.

Erin and the others exchanged perplexed looks.

"Of course." Mr. Ratzka turned to the students. "That was long before your time." He turned back to Doug. "The crawl space was boarded up years ago."

"One of the boards came loose," Doug said. "It looks like it's been loose for a while. It appears Cupid has been spending time there." His smile deepened. "You need to see this."

Miss Pickering stayed in the office with Cupid. The others followed Doug and Mr. Ratzka outside to the east corner of the school. It was the old wing; it had been added on to and renovated many times over the years. It was also close to the service road where school deliveries were made. And workers parked their vehicles.

Doug stopped at a corner overhang, where the old wing joined the new. "See that?" He pointed.

Erin and the others followed the direction of his finger. A series of boards had been nailed together at the base of the building, near the foundation. One of the boards had come loose and slipped, creating a small opening.

Just big enough for a persistent bulldog to wiggle through.

"I was walking to my truck when I heard a scratching, whimpering noise," Doug said. "I immediately went to look." He bent down and retrieved what Erin thought was a large piece of roofing material from the ground. "This had come off, probably from all the banging I'd done earlier. It fell and blocked the access to the opening. Obviously Cupid had gotten inside first and couldn't get out."

Doug tossed the roofing material aside and picked up an industrial-size yellow flashlight. "But what's really interesting is what I found inside the crawl space." He handed the flashlight to Mr. Ratzka. "Take a look."

Erin glanced at her friends. They looked as confused as she was.

Crouching down, Mr. Ratzka beamed the light into the dark space. "Good Lord," he murmured. A funny little smile twisted his lips. "Have a look, Erin."

Erin didn't know what to expect. She exchanged uneasy looks with Rachel and Mona. Then, heart thudding, she bent low and aimed the light into the small crawl space.

At first it looked like a pile of junk. But then she realized. She was looking at Mrs. Abernathy's bracelet. Mr. Ponchet's fountain pen. A watch. The set of keys that had gone missing way back in the beginning. Glasses. A letter opener. And the cell phone that led everyone to think Erin was the Carson Heights thief.

Laughter bubbled up her throat. "It was Cupid," she said, turning to face the others. "Cupid is the Carson Heights thief!"

Chapter Seventeen

RELIEF SWEPT THROUGH Carson Heights after Cupid was found and the Carson Heights thief had been identified. No one was more relieved than Erin. To celebrate, she invited Rachel, Suze, and the others to her place for pizza on Tuesday, the night before the CheeseBarkers competition.

"There's lots more, you guys." Erin said, eyeing the three large pies her dad had picked up. They'd hardly been touched. "Help yourself."

A chorus of polite no thank yous filled Erin's family room. "I'll have another one." Rachel reached for a slice of mushroom-pepperoni. Erin shot her a grateful glance before topping up everyone's soda. It didn't take her long. With seven people crammed into the tiny basement room, the glasses were all within arm's reach.

But the small space was only part of the problem. Erin didn't have a hot tub like Suze, or a surround sound stereo system or a 54-inch HDTV. Even the 2-for-1 pizza from the neighborhood pizzeria wasn't the same. Maybe she should have ordered the more expensive stuff from the place Suze liked.

"How about we play that game Madison brought," Erin suggested. "I'll move the pizzas off the coffee table and we can set it up there."

Madison eyed Erin's coffee table. "That's a pretty small space. And it's a huge board with a pile of pieces and eight boxes of cards. We won't have room."

It *was* a small table, especially compared to the monstrosity in Suze's living room. "We can move into the kitchen then."

Becky and Suze exchanged glances. Madison inspected her fingernails. "I have to go soon." Krista stifled a yawn. "I don't want to get into a game."

Erin had had a momentary twinge of panic when she'd come home from school and told her mother she was having company. What would Suze and the others think of her house? she'd wondered as she'd vacuumed Blue's hair from their worn tweed couch. But she'd let the thought go. She was one of the crowd now. They wouldn't care.

Except they did. And they weren't comfortable at her house, either. Maybe she was expecting too much. It *was* the first time they'd been over. Things would be different after Cupid won tomorrow. Her acceptance by Rachel's new friends would be complete then.

When she glimpsed Suze and Madison rolling their eyes at each other, Erin grew desperate. She shot Rachel a help-me look.

"We need music!" Rachel jumped up and slid the newest Tawp Dawg CD into Erin's player. "And too bad if you don't want to play, Krista, because the rest of us do." She grabbed Madison's game and tipped the board from the box.

The table was small and they did end up with some of the boxed cards on the floor, but the game broke the ice. Pretty soon the girls were laughing and predicting the future and even devouring cold pizza.

"So by this time tomorrow, Carson Heights will be $5,000 richer!" Suze said as the game drew to a close. She gave Madison a high five. "Big party at my place after the competition, remember!"

Erin and Rachel exchanged glances. Going to Suze's place and watching people drink would never make Erin's to-do list. No matter how much she wanted to remain part of the crowd. She'd made that clear to Rachel. But she wasn't about to say anything now. She'd come up with an excuse tomorrow.

"How's Cupid doing anyway?" Becky asked Erin

as they gathered up the game pieces and put them away.

"Pretty good, considering everything he's gone though." Cupid had come through his solitary confinement in the crawl space amazingly well. "I still can't get him to do the slide move consistently, though."

"That's my fault," Suze said with a melodramatic sigh. "If I hadn't gotten creative with the editing, you wouldn't have to worry about it." She touched her hand theatrically to her forehead. "I've just added to your stress."

The other girls giggled. Even Erin smiled. "It's no big deal."

"But what you're going to wear tomorrow is a big deal." Suze grabbed a bag of clothes and began pulling things out. "I brought you a couple more pairs of jeans and three tops. Something should fit." She threw a top and a pair of jeans at Erin. "Try these on."

No way. Erin checked the tag in the jeans. Another size zero. She handed the items back. "Thanks, but I've picked out something to wear."

"Oh." Suze pouted.

"What is it?" asked Krista.

"Something I got last year in Courtenay." She wouldn't admit her *grandmother* had bought it for her.

"Go put it on," Madison urged.

A chorus of voices joined in. Erin dashed upstairs, slipped into the white hipster pants and vest that she loved, and dashed back down again.

"Wow!" Rachel said when Erin appeared in the doorway. "That looks amazing."

"Thanks." Erin felt suddenly shy as Madison and Krista raved about the color, how much older she looked, and how fabulous she'd be dancing on stage.

"It's okay, I guess." Suze tapped her lip and studied Erin thoughtfully. "But...oh, never mind." She waved her red-tipped fingernails in the air. "It's nothing."

"What's nothing?" Erin demanded.

"I don't want to make you self-conscious," Suze said, staring pointedly at Erin's hips. "But white shows every bump."

Erin wanted to shrink into the floor.

"And the pants are kinda short, don't you think?"

The other girls looked down. What was Suze talking about?

"The length is fine." Rachel came to her defense. "Besides, you can always wear flats, right, Erin?"

"Right," Erin agreed.

Madison looked uncertain. "Maybe the jeans would be better."

"Suze is right," Becky chimed in. "White shows everything. Lumps, bumps, and dirt."

"I'll figure it out later," Erin said.

"I'll leave the bag for you then." Suze stood and gathered her things. The others followed suit. "Ratman said you'd be going in his car tomorrow. You're okay if I go with you, aren't you, Erin?"

As long as you're okay if I wear what I want to wear. She just nodded.

"I knew you would be." Suze graced her with another smile. "Thanks for the *great* time! *Love* your place." Her gaze traveled around Erin's family room a little too quickly. "And the pizza was good too. Those cheapy neighborhood places can really cook."

And then she was gone.

—————————— • ⬭

Erin hardly slept at all that night. She was worried about the competition, crushed by Suze's digs about her white pants, and sad that the girls hadn't been comfortable at her house.

"They had a great time," Rachel had said when she'd stayed to help clean up. "What makes you think they didn't?"

Erin didn't bother explaining.

—————————— • ⬭

They were due at the Hyatt Pacific Hotel in downtown Vancouver by 1:00 p.m. Miss Pickering decided to drive Cupid to the hotel in her car. He was used to the vehicle, she said, and if Erin and Deryk came along to help, he'd be fine. The others could go in the school van with Mr. Ratzka. It wasn't what Suze wanted, and Erin knew she'd be upset, but she had more important things to worry about.

Like the media frenzy that greeted them outside the hotel. News vans, camcorders, and boom microphones crowded the valet parking area.

"Dear me," Miss Pickering said as she pulled into the driveway. "Why such a fuss over a little competition?"

A $5,000 prize wasn't exactly little, Erin thought.

"Because of that." Deryk pointed across the street to the line of protesters carrying placards. Erin recognized the PETA logo. "Probably a slow news day," he added.

Richard belonged to PETA—People for the Ethical Treatment of Animals. Erin scanned the signs. Some denounced CheeseBarkers for exploitation while others had crazy slogans like "Feed dogs wheat not meat" and "Pets are people too." Richard would like that one, Erin thought, struggling to control Cupid. The bulldog had taken a fierce and vocal dislike to one of the microphones hanging too close to their car.

"Take him inside," Miss Pickering said. "I'll meet you there."

Deryk grabbed the school camcorder. "Ready?"

Erin wrapped Cupid's leash around her wrist and tucked the bulldog firmly under her arm. "Let's go."

They were peppered with questions as they dashed through the crowd. "Who are you? What's your dog's name? What school are you from? Can you comment on PETA's claims that the Woofer's Corporation is exploiting dogs?"

Deryk fired back answers as they ran, including a terse statement that they had nothing to add to PETA's claim.

"You were good," Erin said when they were inside the lobby and away from the hoards of cameras. "I'm impressed."

He blushed, fiddled with the strap on the camcorder. "My mom's a reporter. Down in L.A. I'm kinda used to the media."

The Hyatt Pacific was one of Vancouver's most upscale hotels. It was filled with Persian carpets, massive chandeliers, and floor-to-ceiling windows that showed Burrard Inlet and the North Shore mountains.

"There's no sign. I guess we should ask for directions," Erin whispered. They headed for the imposing oak reception desk.

"There you are!" yelled a familiar voice. It was

Suze, followed by Mona, Rachel, Zach, and Madison. "Hurry up! They won't let us in without Cupid!"

At the sound of his name, Cupid whined. He wanted down. The staff behind the reception desk glared in their direction.

Deryk rolled his eyes. "Could you be any louder?"

"Shut up, Latham!" Suze grabbed Erin's arm and pulled. "Come on. I want to get inside and see if Tawp Dawg is here!"

Rachel and Mona grinned.

Zach caught Erin's eye. "You look amazing," he said.

Zach thought she looked amazing. So much for Suze's criticisms; Erin was glad she'd made the decision to wear the white pants and vest.

Erin was dragged down a hall and up a flight of stairs to a holding area outside the banquet room. Cupid had to be logged in and given a red and gold ribbon for his collar before they could go inside.

"I don't see Tawp Dawg." Suze gazed around the banquet hall. The stage at one end was empty. People milled around large Woofer's Corporation displays. Erin saw Mr. Ratzka talking to a couple of women, and she saw two dogs—a border collie and a long-haired toy dachshund.

A portly man in a black suit and white shirt waddled toward them. "This must be Cupid from Carson Heights!" With his big stomach and slicked-back hair, he looked like a penguin. "I'm Mr. Scullmoran, Special Events Coordinator and Public Relations Director for the Woofer's Corporation. I'm also head judge of the CheeseBarkers competition."

Head judge. Oh man, what if Cupid lost? Blew it completely?

Mona gave her an encouraging smile; Rachel pressed her hand.

Cupid couldn't blow it. He wouldn't.

Mr. Scullmoran glanced at his clipboard. "Which one of you is Erin Morris?"

"I am." She handed him the CD. "Here's Cupid's music."

He pocketed the disc. "You and the dog will come with me. As for the rest of you, we have a section blocked off for each school. There are signs on the backs of the chairs to guide you." He was about to steer Erin away when he caught sight of Deryk's camcorder. "Are you media?"

"I'm shooting film for our school. I have clearance." Deryk dug into his pocket for the pass he'd received with their orientation package.

"Fine," Penguin Man said. "Just wear your pass,

otherwise you'll be stopped and questioned all afternoon."

"Good luck!" Mona said.

Rachel gave her a quick hug. "Don't worry!" she whispered in her ear. "You'll do fine!"

But would Cupid?

"We're gathering the dogs and their owners back here." Mr. Scullmoran propelled her behind the stage. "I need to have a little chat before we get started." Erin wanted to tell him she wasn't Cupid's owner, but Penguin Man was talking so much she didn't have a chance. "We want to start by 2:00 so we can end by 4:00 and make the dinner-hour news."

Five tables were set up, each with a few chairs and a dog pen nearby. Mr. Scullmoran steered Erin to the closest table. When they were settled, he pointed to a golden retriever in the farthest pen. "That's Maude. She'll go first. Hershey will be second." He pointed to the toy dachshund. "And that's Sadie." He gestured to an Old English sheepdog next to her. "She'll go last. Cupid will perform third."

At the sound of his name, Cupid twisted like a pretzel, wagged his stubby little tail and drooled all over Erin's arm. How embarrassing.

But Mr. Scullmoran appeared charmed. "How delightful you are!" He scratched Cupid behind the ear.

When Cupid snarfed at his hand, he laughed. "I had a bulldog as a youngster. They make wonderful pets."

Feeling a little more relaxed, Erin put Cupid down. She expected him to pull and whine and try to break free from the leash. But he was content to sniff at her feet.

Mr. Scullmoran went over the rules and reminded her that the media would want interviews afterward. "It's all very straightforward," he repeated, removing his black-rimmed glasses and slipping them into his coat pocket. Erin saw Deryk appear, his camcorder doing a sweep of the area. "You won't have any trouble at all."

She hoped not. She really, really hoped not.

"Now." Mr. Scullmoran cleared his throat and leaned forward. "The reality is this. We have already decided which dog we want to sell our product. Which dog will win."

They had? Her heart did a back flip. All that work…all those hours…all that worrying. *For nothing*?

"Who is it?"

He smiled. "That depends on you."

"What do you mean?"

"The trouble with Cupid is he's a little over the top."

"Pardon?" She didn't get it.

He scooped Cupid up, put him on his lap. "The trouble with Cupid is he's a little too jowly here. And a little too droopy here. And his nose fold is a little too deep there." He pinched. He pointed. He probed.

Cupid sat meekly on his lap.

Erin didn't know what shocked her more. Cupid being docile or the plans Mr. Scullmoran had for him.

"We would like to perform surgery. At our expense, of course. Naturally, this must remain *completely* confidential. There's generally a six- to eight-week recovery for this kind of thing, which is not a long time really, not when you consider that the CheeseBarkers mascot must be absolutely perfect."

Erin stared into Cupid's liquid brown eyes, at his lovable muzzle, the ever-present trail of drool trickling down one jowl. Trouble with Cupid? She must have misunderstood. "Did you say surgery?"

"Yes, surgery. In Los Angeles," Mr. Scullmoran clarified. "It's very common and totally low risk. We have an excellent surgeon who does movie stars' pets. You'd be lucky to get Cupid in."

Lucky? There was nothing lucky about it. Cupid didn't need surgery. "What if we say no?" she asked.

Something Erin didn't recognize flickered in his

eyes. "Then we will go with choice number two: Boomer, the English sheepdog. And I can guarantee that a little surgery won't prevent Boomer's owner from saying yes. Our last three dogs have all had surgery, and the owners have been very pleased with the results." He shrugged carelessly. "Dogs are like people. We can all do with a little touch up now and then."

"Why hold a contest?" Erin asked. "If you've already decided?"

"It's good community involvement." Penguin Man put Cupid down. "Good publicity too. Kids in schools across the country know the name CheeseBarkers now. And the media loves a contest. It's a win-win situation."

Win-win. She stared at Cupid. It wouldn't be win-win for him.

Mr. Scullmoran whipped a piece of paper from the back of his clipboard and produced a thick blue pen from the folds of his coat. "If you'll just sign this agreement." He pushed the paper across the table at Erin. "Then we can get on with things."

"I can't," she finally said. "I'm not his owner."

His eyes widened in surprise. "Who is?"

For a split second, Erin considered lying. But her lying days were over. "Miss Pickering," she admitted reluctantly. "Our school secretary. She's out there somewhere. She's the lady with the braided gray hair."

He scooped up his paper and pen. "Feel free to wander around and look at our company displays," he said. "But please put Cupid in the pen. We're trying to keep the mess down."

Keep the mess down?

There was no way she could do that, Erin thought as she watched Penguin Man waddle away.

This mess was way too big to contain.

Chapter Eighteen

THE CHEESEBARKERS contest was a great big scam.

Erin tried to make sense of things. What should she do? Maude the golden retriever began to bark. Cupid whined.

"Don't worry," Erin whispered. "I'm not putting you in any cage."

Miss Pickering would agree to the surgery. It was one of her biggest dreams, having Cupid "touched up." If she'd had the money, she would have done it herself years ago.

And Cupid would win, and Carson Heights would be $5,000 richer, and they'd get a spot in the Tawp Dawg video.

It would all work out.

So why wasn't she happy?

Because Cupid would suffer, just so he'd look better on a can of dog food. And the Woofer's Corporation would make more money. It was exploitation of the worst kind. Richard had been right.

Cupid was restless. He wanted to get off the leash and roam. Pulling a doggie biscuit from her pocket, Erin gave him half. "You didn't even taste that, did you?" she asked after he gulped it down.

He wagged his stubby tail, nudged her hand, and stared up expectantly. "No more!" Seconds later, she broke down and gave him the other half.

She may as well be kind to him now. He'd be going under the knife soon.

Unless she spoke up and told everybody what Penguin Man had said. Erin's heart sped up to triple time.

She could talk to the media, tell everyone the contest was fixed, that the winner had to agree to surgery.

That would save Cupid from the knife.

And blow Carson Height's chances for $5,000. Plus kill their appearance in the Tawp Dawg video.

Erin was in a no-win situation. If she kept her mouth shut, Cupid would face surgery. If she opened her mouth and spoke up, Carson Heights would lose out.

But she would lose out too. Because if she spoke up, if she *blew* it, she'd never be a hero.

It was a no-win situation all right.

"Come on, Cupid, let's go find Mona and Rachel."

Maybe they could help her figure out what to do.

The banquet room was crowded. It took Erin several minutes to find the Carson Heights group, although there was no sign of Miss Pickering and Penguin Man. They were probably talking in a dark corner somewhere.

"I need to talk to you," Erin whispered to Mona. As usual, Rachel was surrounded by people.

"What's wrong?"

"We need to talk and I don't want anyone to hear. Get Rachel and meet me in the bathroom off the lobby." It was far enough away from the banquet room to be safe.

Mona giggled. "Why the secrecy?"

"Trust me. It's important. Don't let anybody know where you're going."

It took Mona and Rachel forever. Luckily the bathroom at the Hyatt Pacific was as deluxe as the lobby and almost as big. Plus, the adjoining powder room featured a tray of sprays and perfumes and lotions. Erin was trying lotion number three when Mona and Rachel finally showed up.

"What's going on?" Rachel asked when she walked through the door. Seeing Cupid sprawled on a loveseat like he owned the place, she added, "You can't have a dog in here."

"Too late. I already do. Besides, the only sign I see is a no-smoking one." Erin gestured to two tiny brass chairs with tapestry covers. "Sit."

She quickly outlined her conversation with Penguin Man, although she had to repeat several parts twice because Rachel, of course, was in total denial that anything bad was going on.

"So now I have to make a decision," Erin said. She glanced at her watch. "In twenty minutes. Because that's when the contest starts."

"They were already calling for dogs and handlers." Mona chewed nervously at the corner of her lip.

"Miss Pickering wouldn't really agree to surgery, would she?" Rachel asked for the third time.

"Take off the rose-colored glasses, Rachel. Of *course* she would. And even if she didn't, someone else would. They've done this for *three years in a row*."

"Can't you let it go?" There was a note of desperation in Rachel's voice. "Just this once?"

Could she? *Should* she?

"It's for a good cause," Rachel urged.

"Not really," Mona countered. "The PETA people are right. It's exploitation."

That's what Richard would say too. Erin stared at Cupid, who was licking his paw and leaving a big, wet spot on the loveseat. He didn't deserve surgery, though he'd probably come through it fine. And Miss Pickering would be thrilled. *Everybody* would be thrilled. She'd be a hero.

Except, it wasn't just about her. It was about the dogs. All of them. The ones that had already had unnecessary surgery. And those that might face it in the future.

Could she forget about them? Win the competition and let people think she was a hero?

She could.

But she wouldn't.

"I can't let this go," Erin said softly. There was a sick, sinking feeling in the pit of her stomach. People were going to be disappointed. But they'd have to live with it. Because if she kept quiet, she wouldn't be able to live with herself. "I have to speak up."

Rachel sighed. "I was afraid you'd say that."

"I'm sorry." Erin braced herself for Rachel's wrath.

But Rachel surprised her. "Yeah, I'm sorry too. Except, knowing how much you care about dogs, I would have been shocked if you'd kept your mouth shut." Her blue eyes reflected both disappointment and acceptance. "It sucks because we'll lose the money, but Cupid is way more important than a stupid old contest. Besides, he doesn't need surgery."

She shot the bulldog a look. "Much." She hesitated. "Do you think we could still get an appearance in that Tawp Dawg video?"

"No!" Erin and Mona said simultaneously.

Rachel grimaced. "You're probably right."

"I just hope Suze and Zach understand," Erin murmured.

"Of course they will! They all love Cupid." Rachel eyed the dog again. "Well, they *like* him at least. And *nobody* would want Cupid to have surgery just to sell some stupid dog food."

There was Rachel's optimism again. For once, Erin prayed her friend was right.

The girls' plan was simple: find Pamela Prendergast, the local TV reporter from CNVC and tell her everything. Unfortunately, the banquet room was mobbed.

"You'll have to make the announcement on stage," Mona said after they'd searched the room twice.

On *stage*? In front of *everybody*?

"We still might find her," Rachel said, seeing the look of horror on Erin's face.

But by the time Maude had finished her routine and they were announcing contestant number two, Hershey the toy dachshund, Erin knew she had no choice.

She had to go up on stage and tell the whole world that the CheeseBarkers competition was a scam. Her panic swelled; she could hardly breathe. Giving that speech over the PA system a few weeks ago had been horrible. How could she speak in front of hundreds of people? Cupid whined; Erin looked into those trusting brown eyes. How could she not?

"Would Erin Morris please report backstage immediately. That's Erin Morris to the backstage area immediately."

"That's the fifth time they've called me! I have to go." Clutching Cupid, she followed Rachel to the side of the stage.

"Just remember, you're doing this for Cupid," Mona said. "And for all the other dogs too."

She was doing this for Cupid. For all dogs.

"There you are!" Miss Pickering ran to her side. She was followed by a frantic-looking Penguin Man. "We were getting worried!" She leaned close, whispered in Erin's ear. "There's nothing to worry about, my dear. Absolutely nothing at all."

That's what you think, Erin wanted to say. Instead, she gave Miss Pickering a halfhearted smile, told Penguin Man she was all set, and waited in the wings for her cue.

"Our third contestant is Cupid the bulldog,"

boomed the announcer, "dancing with Erin Morris from Carson Heights."

Erin could not feel her legs. She could not feel her breath. All she felt was the wild gallop of her heart as she walked to center stage and stared out over the crowd. The music started; the stage shook from the beat. There were eyes everywhere. Staring. Waiting.

Nervously, she wiped her sweaty palms on her white pants. As soon as she opened her mouth, *if* she opened her mouth, there was no going back. She would set in place a chain of events over which she would have no control. Her mother's words floated through her mind.

Lying is easy, the truth is hard.

And this, Erin decided as she opened her mouth and began to talk, was the hardest truth she'd ever had to tell.

"Speak up!" someone yelled.

One of the reporters stuck a microphone in Erin's face. Others followed suit. Scooping Cupid up to keep him safe, Erin outlined her conversation with Mr. Scullmoran and said she agreed with PETA that CheeseBarkers was exploiting animals.

At some point, the music died. That's when Cupid got really restless, jumped down, and ran to

Miss Pickering. That's when Erin caught sight of the sea of disappointed faces beside the stage. The whole Carson Heights group. And she was letting them down.

But she couldn't think about it. Instead, she kept talking and answering questions until, finally, the reporters hurried off to find Mr. Scullmoran and the questions stopped.

"You did great!" Mona said when she came off-stage.

Rachel gave her a fierce hug. "That took guts!"

"Where is everybody?" The wings of the stage had been crowded with people when she'd been talking; now they were deserted.

"The media are doing interviews," Mona said.

"You're a star!" Rachel added excitedly. "I heard the guy from Global say this story's huge. Apparently Tawp Dawg is big into animal rights. They're probably going to pull sponsorship from CheeseBarkers and the Woofer's Corporation."

Erin didn't know whether that made her feel better or worse. "I have to find Miss Pickering." She led Rachel and Mona backstage. "She's going to be really upset over this."

Mr. Scullmoran was standing beside one of the cages, being interviewed by a group of reporters.

Mona saw him first. She grabbed Erin's arm; the three girls came to a sudden, silent stop.

"It's simply not true." Even though he had his back to them, Erin heard every word. "CheeseBarkers has never advocated unnecessary surgery."

Rachel and Erin exchanged wide-eyed looks.

"Any dog that appears on our dog food is the way nature made them," he continued. "That girl is clearly making the whole thing up. Besides, why would I talk to her about surgery anyway? She's not even Cupid's owner."

"Let's get out of here," Mona hissed.

"I never expected him to *lie* about it," Erin said when they were safely out of the backstage area and in the banquet room. Tears stung behind her eyes. She'd given up $5,000 and an appearance in a Tawp Dawg video for animal rights. What if she'd done it for nothing?

"Don't worry," Rachel said. "He approached Miss Pickering too, remember? She'll tell the truth."

The crowd had thinned, but there were still enough people that it was hard to find their group. "I see Miss Pickering over there." Mona pointed toward the door.

They hadn't gone three steps when Pamela

Prendergast swooped down on them. "I've been looking for you!" She laid a hand on Erin's arm. "Don't go anywhere. Don't move!" She cast a wild look over her shoulder. "Bill," she called. "Bill, over here!"

"At least now you can set the record straight," Mona whispered when the burly cameraman appeared and switched on his light.

Rachel gave her the thumbs-up sign. Erin wiped her clammy hands on her pants.. Mona was right; she could tell her side of the story again.

"Can you comment on the fact that Cheese-Barkers and the Woofer's Corporation insists your statement is simply not true?" Pamela Prendergast asked.

Erin wouldn't look into the camera. Instead, she spoke directly to Pamela, repeating almost word for word that she'd said on stage.

When Erin was finished, the woman gave her a frozen smile. "We have it on authority from your schoolmates that you make up stories, that you don't always tell the truth."

The bottom dropped out of Erin's stomach. "What?"

Pamela flipped open her notebook, rifled through some pages, began to read. "Erin is a liar.

She always makes up stories." She flipped the note-book shut, gave a little shrug. "Two people said it. Care to comment?"

Rachel spoke instead. "I don't believe you."

But Erin did. It was Suze. She was mad and she was striking back. Madison or Becky had probably backed her up like they always did. What a mess. A lone tear snaked its way down her cheek. All she'd wanted to do was make sure dogs weren't being exploited.

Pamela's face softened. "Let me play you the tape. You need to know what's being said, because every reporter in this place wants to talk to you."

The cameraman flipped off his light; Erin, Rachel, and Mona crowded around his machine. "Watch the screen," he said.

It was a tiny monitor, the size of a large man's palm. But it played the images clearly. Erin wasn't surprised when Suze appeared. But she just about fell over when Zach appeared beside her.

Zach Cameron was the second person?

"Erin is a liar," Suze said. "She always makes up stories. This is just another one of her stories, right, Zach?"

Zach gazed into the camera, his gold-flecked brown eyes wide and honest-looking. "Absolutely," he said. "Just a few weeks ago, she made up a crazy story about some imaginary friend named Lola. It's the kind of thing she does. You can't believe her. Carson Heights deserves another chance. We deserve to compete in this competition. We deserve to win that $5,000."

You can't believe her.

Zach had sold her out. He'd made Erin sound like a fool. All because he wanted Carson Heights to win.

Somehow, Erin wasn't surprised. She'd noticed things for weeks. Only she'd been too stupid, too *love struck,* to pay attention. Now she had to face the truth: Zach Cameron wasn't the guy she thought he was.

Talk about disappointments. First the Cheese-Barkers competition. And now Zach.

"I can't believe they said that," Rachel kept repeating. "I just can't believe it!" She asked Pamela Prendergast to play the conversation a second time.

"They're making you out to be the bad guy," Rachel said to Erin after it ended. She looked dazed.

"Surprise, surprise!" Erin said dryly.

"All this time you kept telling me about Suze and I didn't believe you." The corner of her mouth trembled.

Erin knew Rachel was on the verge of tears. But if she broke down, Erin would too. And she wanted to grieve her losses in private. "Rachel, it's okay. Don't worry about it. We'll talk about it later."

"Yeah, right now we have to figure out what to do," Mona said.

Mona's words snapped Rachel back to attention. She stared at the two of them for a minute and then said, "I know exactly what to do. Roll that tape," she ordered, tossing her blonde hair over her shoulder. "I have something to say."

The light went back on; the camera began to whir. And Rachel spoke. "I've known Erin Morris since grade two and she is totally honest. She always does the right thing, and she always tells the truth, even when it's hard." Rachel had stopped trembling, and though she was rushing to get her point across, her voice was clear and strong. "Yes, she made up a story about an imaginary friend named Lola. Because I bullied her into it. It was a stupid joke and it backfired and maybe we shouldn't have done it, but it's over and it doesn't take away from the fact that if Erin said CheeseBarkers insisted on plastic surgery, then that's what happened. Suze Shillington and Zach Cameron are twisting things around because they're lousy losers."

"Whoa," Mona murmured under her breath. "That's big."

It was bigger than big, Erin thought as Pamela Prendergast quizzed Rachel. It was also a new beginning. She'd lost her illusions where Zach was concerned, and she knew she'd never be part of the in crowd either. But she'd gotten her best friend back. Because now Rachel saw what Suze was really like. And she'd stood up for Erin in spite of it.

"Unfortunately," Pamela said as her conversation with Rachel drew to a close, "it comes down to one person's word against another's."

"No it doesn't," came a voice from behind.

It was Deryk Latham.

Chapter Nineteen

"So DERYK HAD THE WHOLE conversation on tape," Erin explained to her parents later that night as they sat in the family room eating Chinese food. "I guess he zoomed in on the conversation when Mr. Scullmoran was talking to me. And when he played it back, Mr. Scullmoran couldn't deny it anymore."

"Deryk sure stayed calm," Rachel said, helping herself to more chicken fried rice.

"Yeah, the media rushed him after he made the announcement and it didn't faze him a bit," Mona added.

"His mom's a reporter down in Los Angeles," Erin explained. "Apparently he's used to the press." She slipped Blue a piece of stir-fried beef and pretended not to see her father's look of disapproval.

"What about Miss Pickering?" Erin's mom asked. She put her plate on the coffee table, leaned against the old tweed couch, and rubbed her stomach.

"She wasn't too happy." Erin let Blue lick her fingers before wiping them clean on a napkin. "But we didn't have time to talk. She wanted to get Cupid home."

"She's bound to be disappointed," Erin's father said. "But—"

The ringing phone interrupted him.

He groaned. "Don't make me get up again. It'll be for you anyway."

The phone hadn't stopped ringing since Erin had arrived home. News of the CheeseBarkers scam had hit both radio and television. Erin was considered a hero for speaking out.

Too bad she wasn't the kind of hero she'd dreamed of being.

"Hello," she said into the receiver.

"Is this Erin Morris?"

The accented voice was strangely familiar, yet Erin couldn't place it. "Yes, this is she," she said primly.

Rachel giggled; Erin booted her in the thigh.

"This is Caden Vaughan from Tawp Dawg."

Erin put her hand over the receiver. "It's some guy saying he's Caden Vaughan from Tawp Dawg."

Rachel snickered. "It's probably Anthony. You know how he likes to play practical jokes."

That's why the voice sounded so familiar.

Rachel yelled in the direction of the receiver. "Cut it out, Anthony, we know it's you. Erin's in big demand. We need to leave the phone clear for the reporters who want to get through."

"Are you expecting a call?" the voice asked.

Erin giggled. "Anthony, your Welsh accent stinks! Of *course* I'm expecting a call. I'm expecting a zillion calls. Wanna talk to Rachel?"

"Do you live at 345 East 9th?"

Erin snorted. "No, we moved since yesterday. Give it up, Anthony. We know it's you."

"Look out your window, I'm in a white limo."

Erin rolled her eyes. "Yeah, and I'm Caden Vaughan's girlfriend." She put her hand over the receiver. "He says I should look out the window because he's in a white limo."

"Would it be all right if I stopped in?"

"He wants to know if it would 'be all right if he stopped in?'" Erin mimicked Anthony's fake Welsh accent.

Everybody laughed. "Tell him there's enough Chinese food left," her mother said.

"Uh, Erin?" Mona had gone to the window. When she turned back, there was a funny look on her face. "There's a white limo parked in front of your house."

"No way!"

"Yes, way."

They rushed to the window; Blue began to bark.

"That thing's huge." Her mother was right; it stretched way past their front yard.

Erin's hand started to shake. "I don't believe this." Now her arm was shaking, her legs were shaking, her *whole body* was shaking. "This can't be happening."

The voice on the other end of the phone laughed. "I take it I have the right house," it said.

The door to the limo opened; Caden Vaughan stepped onto the sidewalk, grinned, and waved in their direction.

And that's when Rachel screeched, "My God, it's him!"

Right before she fainted on the family room floor.

"You aren't going to faint again, are you?" Erin gave Rachel a nervous look.

"Of course I'm not going to faint," Rachel said as she helped herself to another soda from the limo's mini bar.

Rachel was only pretending to be cool and calm. How could she be when they really *were* riding through Stanley Park in the Tawp Dawg limo? And inside, there really *were* three phones, two televisions, and enough food for twenty.

Caden Vaughan really *had* come to her house.

It was so hard to believe.

Lately, her whole life was one big fairy tale, right down to the fact that Tawp Dawg had agreed to perform at their spring dance. In less than an hour.

When Caden Vaughan had offered Erin the limo and told her to invite some friends for a ride before the dance, naturally she'd invited Rachel, Mona, Anthony, and Joseph. But she'd invited Deryk Latham too. He'd saved her life at the Cheese-Barkers competition. If it wasn't for him, people still might not believe her. Besides, she thought, sneaking a glance sideways, inviting him wasn't exactly a hardship. He'd gotten that new haircut and lately he'd been dressing better. Tonight, he wore black jeans and a tight beige T-shirt that made his blue eyes stand out.

"Man, you could hold a football game in here," Anthony said from three seats away. "This thing's huge."

"Don't get any ideas," Erin warned as the limo left the park and merged onto the Lions Gate Bridge.

Mona and Joseph laughed. Deryk smiled and offered Erin some chips.

She took a handful and smiled back. "Thanks." She stared out the window to the freighters in the water below. They chugged through the inlet, past the strip of sand on Ambleside Beach. They were on a mission to unload their cargo. The limo was on a mission too. Delivering them to Carson Heights.

"Look at that crowd," Mona said a few minutes later when the limo turned up the street to Carson Heights.

"Caden, Caden!" The crowd rushed the limo as it pulled up in front of the school.

Deryk grinned. "So this is what it feels like to be a star."

"I could get used to it," Anthony joked as he and Rachel made their way to the limo's doors.

When the doors opened, camera flashes blinded them. Erin grabbed her purse, smoothed her new jeans, and stepped out. A sigh of disappointment swept through the crowd. "It's not Caden!" someone yelled.

"Caden's already inside." Erin repeated what she'd been told to say. "He was brought in through a secret access and he'll leave the same way." She flashed a grin. "He said to say hi to everybody, though."

Those attending the dance quickly turned and rushed for the school. The rest of the crowd seemed to deflate all at once. Slowly, people broke into groups and trickled away. Erin heard one girl proclaim, "I don't care what she says; there are only so many ways in and out of this school. I'm staying here until the dance is over, just in case he comes out."

Good for her, Erin thought as they headed for the gym. Maybe she'd be lucky and she would see Caden Vaughan.

Life was full of surprises.

"Erin, we've been waiting for you!" Suze rushed up. "I love your new jeans."

Deryk gave Suze a look of disgust before joining Anthony and Joseph.

"Thanks," Erin said coolly. Madison, Becky, and Krista chimed in with their approval too. They were like clones. If Suze approved of something, they all did.

And since word was out that Caden Vaughan had shown up at Erin's house, Suze approved of anything Erin said, did, or wore. "Any chance we could all go backstage after the dance?" She tucked her arm through Erin's.

"I don't think so." Erin pulled her arm away and picked up her pace. The less time she spent with Suze and her crowd, the better.

Suze hurried right along beside her. "Why don't I hang around with you, just in case?"

"Why don't you *not*," Rachel snapped.

"Be nice," Erin murmured.

Rachel was still angry at herself for having encouraged Erin to be Suze's friend. And she was disillusioned too, now that she knew what Suze was really like. She couldn't believe she'd been fooled.

Disillusionment was tough, Erin reflected when she stepped inside the gym and heard a familiar laugh. The room was only dimly lit, but it didn't matter. It was Zach's laugh. She'd dreamed it enough times to know. Still, when she turned and saw him flipping his hair away from those tawny brown eyes, a tiny ping erupted in the region of her heart. Disillusionment wasn't only tough but it also hurt.

"Ladies and gentlemen," boomed Mr. Ratzka from the stage. "Make sure your friends are inside. We'll be shutting the doors and locking them in five minutes."

A roar went up from the crowd. "Caden, Caden!"

Erin and Rachel exchanged grins. Rachel was the only one who knew the announcement that was coming. Well, other than her parents, of course. She hadn't told Mr. Ratzka or Miss Pickering. She hadn't even told Mona.

"Erin, my dear, I'm glad I found you." It was Miss Pickering, all decked out in her black suit and smelling of her familiar lavender perfume. "Please give this to your mother as a thank-you for watching Cupid." She thrust a small, gold-wrapped box into Erin's hand.

"She doesn't mind," Erin said. "You don't need to give her a gift."

"Now, now," the older woman said. "It's the least I can do."

Erin slipped the package into her purse. Miss Pickering claimed Cupid didn't like being alone since getting trapped in the crawl space. Erin's mother had offered to go to Miss Pickering's house and sit with him for a few hours.

"Are you excited?" Mona asked the school secretary.

"Excited isn't the word for it!" Miss Pickering laid a hand on her heart. "Do you know, that nice boy Caden autographed *four* pictures, one for each of my great-nieces?" Erin, Rachel, and Mona nodded. They knew, all right. Miss Pickering had talked about it all week. "And he also told me what *really* goes on in Los Angeles." She dropped her voice, leaned close. "I'm telling you, girls, everyone is getting plastic surgery these days. Eeevery one." They knew this too, but they pretended to be hearing it for the first time. "But like Caden says, that doesn't make it right. Not at all. Especially not for dogs."

Erin had been both amused and relieved when she heard about the conversation between Caden Vaughan and Miss Pickering. The Welsh singing sensation had achieved something Erin hadn't been able to—he'd talked Miss Pickering out of plastic surgery for Cupid.

Mr. Ratzka was back onstage, fiddling with the microphone.

"It's starting!" Rachel said. "Come on. Let's go find Anthony."

Anthony was with Joseph and Deryk. As the girls joined them, Mr. Ratzka announced, "Ladies and gentleman, please put your hands together for Tawp Dawg!"

The curtain opened; the spotlights blinked on. The crowd erupted. And Tawp Dawg broke into song:

> *Feed me luv, in any way you can.*
> *Feed me luv, I'll be at your command.*
> *I'll be your slaveman,*
> *Your caveman,*
> *Your Superman*
> *Through the rest of time.*
> *If you'll just feed me, feed me, feed me luv.*

Erin and Mona exchanged grins. Boy, did they know that song inside out. No one danced, not at first.

Instead, people stood swaying and clapping in time to the beat. After the final chorus, Caden Vaughan stepped forward. "Hello, Carson Heights!" he yelled.

"Hello!" the crowd boomed back.

"Are we gonna rock tonight?"

"Yeah!" everyone shouted.

Caden Vaughan cupped his hand behind his ear. "I can't hear you!"

"YEAH!" the crowd bellowed.

Erin put her hands over her ears; Deryk laughed.

"Before we get down to some serious rocking, I have an important announcement to make."

"Just sing, man!" someone shouted.

Caden Vaughan's grin deepened. "Oh, we're gonna sing. Don't worry."

Erin couldn't take her eyes from him. *He* had been in her living room. *He* had shaken her hand. *He* had given her one of the best compliments she had ever received.

She still had trouble believing it.

"Carson Heights recently lost out on $5,000." There was a collective groan. "But you lost out for a good cause." The groan deepened. Mona sent Erin a worried look. Even Deryk glanced in her direction.

"You lost because Erin Morris stood up for the rights of animals. It was a hard decision for her to make, because she knew she was letting her friends down. But she did it for the greater good. Most people would have caved under the pressure. I admire her guts." Scattered clapping broke out here and there. "As you may or may not know, we decided to play here tonight in honor of Erin Morris."

The clapping grew stronger; Erin blushed. She hadn't expected him to say *that*.

"We're also leaving a check for $5,000 with your Special Events Committee because we think Cupid is a winner and Carson Heights is a winner too, no matter what the Woofer's Corporation says."

The crowd erupted into a hurricane of cheers, claps, whistles, and shouts.

Mona hugged her. Rachel did too. Deryk gave her a high-five. The announcement was like a little jolt of electricity. Even though she'd been expecting it, Erin still couldn't quite believe Tawp Dawg was giving their school $5,000.

"And we're also making a donation to Erin Morris's favorite charity—the SPCA. Instead of $5,000, we're giving them $10,000 because somebody has to stand up for the animals." He slammed out a cord; the crowd roared.

"What?" Erin couldn't have heard right. Shocked, she stared at the stage, then back at her friends.

"Did he just say he was donating ten grand to the SPCA?"

"He did!" Rachel said.

"Whoa!" Erin's knees started to shake. Wait'll Richard heard this.

"And now!" Caden Vaughan yelled as he strummed his guitar. "Let's rock!"

Some people broke into pairs, started dancing. Others came up and spoke to Erin. She accepted their congratulations in a bit of a daze. Ten thousand dollars to the SPCA? *Plus* $5,000 to Carson Heights?

"Hey, Erin. Way to go." It was Zach.

"Thanks."

He bounced gently from one foot to the other; his cheeks were tinged with pink. Erin could tell he was embarrassed. He hadn't spoken to her since the CheeseBarkers competition.

"I guess…ah…like everybody says, doing the right thing paid off."

"I guess." Out of the corner of her eye, she saw Deryk glowering. He'd told her more about the digging fiasco at his house last summer. Zach had brought beer, and when Deryk's father came home unexpectedly, Deryk had gotten into a whack of trouble because Zach had refused to take responsibility. Erin wasn't surprised.

"Uh...wanna dance?" Zach asked.

He still had gorgeous eyes and that killer smile. That would never change. But Zach Cameron wasn't a God after all. He was just a guy with a weak character. Suze had said it best: Zach always took the easy way out. And Erin's days of taking the easy way out were over.

"Sorry," she said, walking up to Deryk and taking his hand. "I promised this dance to someone else."